KEEPER OF THE LIGHT

Saint Macrina the Elder, Grandmother of Saints

by Bev. Cooke
illustrated by Bonnie Gillis

Ancient Faith Publishing
Chesterton, Indiana

KEEPER OF THE LIGHT
Saint Macrina the Elder, Grandmother of Saints

Text copyright © 2006 by Bev. Cooke
Illustrations copyright © 2006 by Bonnie Gillis

Published by   Ancient Faith Publishing
(formerly known as Conciliar Press)
P.O. Box 748
Chesterton, IN 46304

Printed in the United States of America

ISBN 978-1-888212-77-8

Contents

Key to the words listed in the glossary:
The glossary provides definitions for a number of Latin and historical terms. These terms appear in **_bold italic_** type the first time they are used in the text.

To my family:
Al, Arwen, and Mark
James
Donna, Lawrence, Rhiannon, and Magdalen
Mavis.
You are my heart.

And to the memory of my parents:
Selwyn and Peggy
Memory Eternal.
I wish I could hand you this book
and see your expressions.

Acknowledgments

WRITERS PUT THE WORDS ON THE PAGE in isolation, tucked away with pen & paper or keyboard, but they're never really alone. God and the angels and saints surround them, and behind them are the people who encourage them, support them, and put up with the emotional rollercoaster that is the journey from idea to printed book.

The family suffers most. Al, Arwen, and Mark believed in me, hugged me, made me coffee, and put up with a wife and mother who may have been there in the body, but sure wasn't in mind most of the time. I love you. Thank you for being my family.

Mavis Andrews and Matushka Donna Farley are my sisters of the heart as well as of the pen, and I could never have become the author of this book without them. I don't think I could have remained a writer without their love and encouragement through all the years. Thank you doesn't even begin to cover it!

Father Lawrence Farley provided translations from the Septuagint, and gently encouraged and supported me as much as his wife did. He answered historical and theological questions and shored me up during crises of confidence with good humor, gentleness, and patience. He taught me far more than the ancient Christian faith. He teaches me about timeless Christian love and belief every day.

My critique group: Margot and Joe, Sheila and Jan. Despite differing religious beliefs, they treated the book and my beliefs with respect, gentleness, and love. They demanded that I honor my faith through my work. They never accepted less than my best. As a result both the book and I are better than I ever thought we could be. Thank you so much!

To Ginny, Jane, Katherine, Shelly, and Carla—editors at Conciliar who did such a magnificent job of producing the book you are holding: thank you for believing in me and working with me, and being even prouder of this than I am.

And I owe a thank-you to my dance teacher, Lynda Raino. Her dedication and heart inspired me and kept me going when I was certain I'd never be published. She's an utterly incredible dancer and a wonder to watch.

Saints Macrina the Elder and the Younger. I'm still not sure how I began writing about my name saint's grandmother, but they interceded for me during the writing. My humble and grateful thanks for their prayers.

Thanks and gratitude most of all to God: Father, Son, and Holy Spirit. "Meet it is at all times to worship You with voices of praise, O Son of God and Giver of life." I pray this book, small and unworthy as it is, is an acceptable voice of praise to You, O Gracious Redeemer. Glory to God for all things!

Section One
In Exile

T he hammering on the door wakened Macrina.
"Open in the name of the Emperor Diocletian!" a deep harsh voice shouted. She gasped and
leaped out of bed as an even louder and heavier crash
boomed through the house.

"Get *Mus*, I'll get the pack," said Basil, her husband,
as he darted out of the room.

She grabbed her *palla* on the way out and raced

through the upper floor of the house. Downstairs, she heard the front door slam open and rough, loud voices echo through the rooms.

Skidding around a corner and through the doorway, she slid to a stop by her son's bed. The glow from her husband's lamp as he reached the door behind her banished a little of her terror along with the darkness.

Basil fidgeted in the doorway, his bow slung over his shoulder, and the always-prepared pack on his back. Besides some money and food, changes of clothing and odd bits and pieces, the pack was home for the relics of her spiritual father, Bishop Gregory, copies of letters from the early church fathers, and the sacred writings.

"Basil, little Mus, wake up now." It was hard to speak soothingly to the confused six-year-old, to move slowly and gently when all her being told her just to grab her husband's hand, snatch up her son, and flee. "Wake now, son. Time to get up."

"What?" he asked sleepily. "Why?"

"It's soldiers, sweet boy," Macrina whispered as she gathered him in her arms. "They've come to arrest us because we're Christian. You must be as quiet as a mouse," she said.

"Because I'm little like one," the child muttered.

"And because you can be as quiet as one when you want. And now you must be." She held him close and the strong, smooth beat of his heart steadied her. She nodded at her husband. They clambered out the window, onto the tile roof of the *atrium*.

The crack of furniture breaking and smash of pottery and dishes that rose from the central, open roof announced the soldiers' progress through the house. The cries and screams of the servants as they were pulled from bed tore at Macrina's heart. She paused and turned toward the noise. Her husband, the elder Basil, grabbed her arm.

"We can't—we don't dare let them get the relics and the writings," he whispered.

She nodded and clung to his arm as they moved quietly along the roof around the garden to the road at the back of the house. Once on the ground they sped through the sleeping streets of Neocaesarea.

The cool, smooth stone underfoot gave way to hard-packed earth, then damp, springy loam as they ran through the cleared fields into the forest beyond town. Here, their progress was more difficult, for the overarching trees hid the light of the moon, and the scrubby undergrowth grabbed at their clothing.

They ran until she collapsed, chest heaving, sweat streaming down her face and her legs trembling. She held her son close as she panted for air. Basil collapsed beside her. Macrina dabbed at the bloody scratches the thorny undergrowth had left on her arms and Mus' legs.

"Mama, where are we going?" Her son twisted in her arms as she wrapped her red palla, the long rectangular cloth that served as a combination cloak and shawl, around them both. She was glad she'd grabbed it, although she couldn't remember doing so. It was early spring and the nights were still cold.

"We'll find a lovely hiding place in the morning. With a cave and some water, and lots to eat. But we're safe now, so you can sleep."

Six was a bit old to be cuddled like an infant, but Mus made no protest and wrapped his arm around her neck as she shifted him on her lap and rocked him, singing in a low, soothing voice, "O Gladsome Light of the holy glory, of the immortal Father . . ."

"It's night, not evening," murmured Mus.

Macrina pointed. Through a gap in the trees they glimpsed stars twinkling and clouds scudding across a sky as black as their future seemed.

"Look, there's a full moon, just come from behind a cloud. And we can still glorify Him, and ask for protection," she said.

Once the child was asleep, Basil tied his son to Macrina's back.

"Do you know where we are?" she asked him in a low voice.

He heaved the pack up from the ground and slung it on his back. "I think so. But we can't stay here. It's too close to town. We'll have to keep going and find a well-hidden spot. Carry the lamp for me." He enfolded Macrina and the sleeping boy in his arms. "Whatever happens, God is with us, Macrina. Hold to that."

He was right, Macrina thought as they set off. She wondered which of their friends hadn't been able to get away, who hadn't wakened in time to run, how many houses were empty today.

Had Claudia, her oldest and best friend, escaped with her husband, Flavius? Or had someone finally revealed their secret? *Please God,* she thought, *let them be safe. Let us be safe—protect us all, and be with those who weren't able to run.*

There was no wondering about what would happen to those poor souls. Nearly three hundred years of persecution had taught the Christians exactly what kind of treatment they could expect from Rome.

Macrina and Basil walked until dawn, when they stopped by a stream for a bite to eat. Once Mus woke, they made a quiet game with him of finding the least overgrown paths and clearest animal trails. His eyes were sharp and he found more than both his parents together. It was slow, hard work. They moved forward, only to be blocked by a deadfall, or undergrowth so thick they couldn't push their way through.

By sunset, they were exhausted from the exertion and the sudden halts to hide when they thought they heard soldiers.

Macrina stumbled into a clearing behind her husband. Off to one side, by a walnut tree, an outcrop of rock and a dark shadow hinted at a cave.

"Could we stay here?" she asked. She dug her knuckles into the small of her back and stretched over them as Basil poked around the rock outcropping.

He disappeared, and a moment later, his muffled voice drifted into the clearing. "Come see, Macrina, Basil."

It was gloomy inside, but enough light filtered in for her to see a space that would barely accommodate the three of them. The dry, sandy floor was level, but an abundance of small rocks and lumps made Macrina grimace. She didn't relish the idea of sleeping on tree roots.

Her men poked around in the back of the cave, and in a moment, little Basil scampered out of the gloom.

"It's perfect, Papa says. We can stay here! Isn't this exciting? I want to explore."

Without waiting for permission, he dashed outside. Macrina sprang to her feet, exhaustion forgotten. She had no idea how far they were from Neocaesarea, and none of them were gifted in the ways of woodcraft. If soldiers didn't get him, wild animals might.

She burst into the clearing, then relaxed. Mus was playing in the last, dappled sunlight, oblivious to any danger from man or beast. She crossed herself and blew a sigh in relief, then returned to the cave to unpack their few belongings while Basil hid the relics and writings, and inscribed a cross on the outside wall of their new home.

Chapter Two
Summer 304

Macrina laughed and scooped some water from the stream, then threw it at her son. He squealed and dashed toward her, splashing like a brace of clumsy oxen.

"You don't fight fair!" she yelled.

"It's more fun to splash with your legs," Mus retorted. He jumped toward her and the resultant wall of water soaked her from the thighs down. She turned and ran upstream, glancing over her shoulder to make sure she didn't get too far ahead.

A wet smack, a solid body hitting her as Mus tackled her, and they both landed full-length in the water. Tumbling through the water, they wriggled like eels, and screamed with laughter.

A shadow fell over them and they stopped, looking up in sudden fear, but it was only Basil, back from hunting. He held a rabbit by its ears.

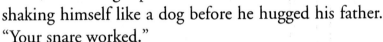

"You finally got one, Papa!" seven-year-old Mus cried, climbing up and shaking himself like a dog before he hugged his father. "Your snare worked."

Basil looked pleased with himself, and he greeted Macrina with a kiss as she stood in the stream and smoothed her wet, black hair away from her face.

"Thanks be to God that I remembered what old Marcus taught me. If he were here now, he'd box my ears for forgetting so much."

Mus giggled at the thought of someone boxing his tall, stately father's ears. "But you did remember, so he wouldn't."

"Good thing, too, or I wouldn't have caught anything," the hunter said. "But we have rabbit for supper. If Mama can figure out how to cook it."

Macrina eyed the dead creature. So far, most of their diet had consisted of greens and fish. She'd mastered cooking the fish, but this!

Basil laughed at her expression. "I can skin and clean it for you," he said. "I'll even cut it up. But—"

He stopped and cocked his head. Suddenly uneasy, Macrina took her son by the hand.

"Papa—"

Basil held a hand up, indicating he needed quiet, and in a moment, Macrina heard the voices—too far to make out words, but it sounded like one giving orders and the others acknowledging. Before Mus could form another question, she scooped him up and ran for the clearing.

It didn't take long to gather their possessions and stuff them into the pack. She didn't bother with the bowls and spoons they'd been teaching themselves to carve, there was no time. Even as she grabbed her palla and Basil's *toga*, she could hear the shouted voices coming closer.

How could they have become so careless, she chided herself. They'd been here over a year, and it felt like home—an excursion into the wilderness for fun, not as though they were hiding for their lives.

Basil tossed the rabbit into the bushes, tucked the relics and writings into the pack, slung it on his back and grabbed Mus's hand. They dashed along faint animal paths, jumped deadfalls, and ducked under low-lying limbs.

The sun had reached its zenith before they paused to catch their breath. Once their panting slowed, they listened intently.

Birdsong, animal chatter, and small rustlings, along with the breeze in the treetops. Then, voices, louder than they'd been at the cave. The pursuers were close enough that Macrina could hear the crunch and rustle of the bush as the men moved toward the family. Groaning silently, she turned and ran after her husband.

Basil crashed through the brush, Mus in his arms,

19

breaking trail for Macrina. She could see his grubby tunic ahead, hear the harsh panting—then, with a yell, he disappeared. Before she could stop herself, Macrina too plunged over the edge and fell into the river.

Sputtering, coughing, and shaken, Macrina flailed around until her hand encountered warm flesh. Basil's hand grabbed her and hauled her to her feet. Basil glanced over his shoulder, to make sure she was following, then headed up-river.

She pushed her sopping hair out of her eyes and scraped her hands over her face to wipe the water off as she followed Basil up the thigh-deep river.

"We'll—stay in the—river," he panted, once she'd caught up to him.

"Then pray the river bends soon," she replied. Basil nodded and they waded on. It made sense to stay in the water as long as they could. There was no dirt or dried needles to take their footprints, no dead leaves and undergrowth to rustle and betray their movements, or twigs and branches to break and mark their passage. No thorny bushes to catch bits of clothing. No trail—just the fast rushing river, parting as they moved and closing behind them. Any noise they made was covered by the rush and tumble of the water itself.

Little Basil understood the seriousness and the need for quiet, even if he didn't know the cause, and said nothing until they'd traveled a considerable distance.

"Are they soldiers?" he asked finally.

Macrina nodded, grim-faced. It had finally dawned on her that this might not be a prolonged wilderness trip, but a way of life. Did God mean for them to become recluses and hermits, wandering the mountains forever and praising Him? She hoped not. She could do it, if God demanded it, but it would be hard to be cheerful and submissive to His will, if that is what He asked.

The river did bend, finally, and bent again, further on. They walked past sunset, through twilight, stumbling over rocks and falling into the water, tripping on dead tree branches and bashing their heads on low-hanging limbs.

The one comfort, Macrina reflected as she picked herself up, was that the soldiers, if they were still following, would be as slow and clumsy as themselves in the light of the half moon.

And that her tunic would be thoroughly rinsed, if not clean.

When she fell again, Basil called a halt for the night.

They left the river and stumbled their way to a small clear spot far enough from the water to be able to hear anyone or anything approach. Mus had long since fallen asleep in his father's arms, and Macrina took only seconds to follow her son.

By the third day in the river, Macrina was convinced her feet were growing scales.

She sighed. "Can we stop soon?" she asked her husband, as the sun sank behind the trees. "We're hungry, and tired."

He nodded. "As soon as we find a likely spot. Keep an eye out for one. Water, a small clear area, that's all we need."

"A fire?"

He thought about it, then shook his head. "It's too risky. They can see and smell the smoke for miles. It won't be long until dark, and the flame will show too clearly. Tomorrow perhaps, if it seems safe we'll leave the water and look for a good spot to stay. If they haven't caught up with us by now, then perhaps they've given up."

Macrina no longer knew if the soldiers were still on their trail. All she wanted to do was sit and not move, ever again.

Chapter Three
Autumn 306–Autumn 307

"Mama," called Mus, as they trekked along a mountain trail in the fourth autumn of their exile, "my shoe." He stopped and held up his foot. Dangling from his toes was the foul-smelling, tattered remnant of Basil's latest attempt at cobbling.

She nodded. They moved off the trail into a tiny clearing at the edge of a cliff. As they buried the shoe, to avoid anyone finding it and trailing them, Macrina noticed smoke rising from the valley.

She moved to the edge of the clearing, brushed her dirty, tangled hair back from her face and looked down to the river, about a hundred feet below them.

"There, Basil, see? A town." Macrina pointed down into the valley. Set by a river, no barracks apparent, huddled a small town. The road leading in was well kept, and the presence of docks told Basil and Macrina that trade boats stopped there.

"We'll go higher," Basil replied, turning from the edge of the cliff and moving toward the trees.

"But please, let's go down and find out if we can go home," she said.

"Macrina, you know the danger. There probably isn't a Christian in the entire village. You know most of us are city folk."

"But there aren't any soldiers, and we could get away if anyone finds out. And why would they? Look at us! We surely don't look like ourselves. Look at my skin— I'm as brown as a field slave. Look at Mus's tunic. I've patched it so often it looks like a slave's castoff, and he's outgrown it so I can't lengthen it anymore. Yours is so dingy it's almost black. We don't have anything to show we're Christian!"

"And if we arrive on a pagan feast day? Look—that's a temple. We'd be expected to sacrifice, and then they'd know. It doesn't look like a rich village, and I'm sure the Emperor would pay handsomely for us. No. It's not worth the risk."

"Not even to buy some fabric, or some shoes?"

"No, Macrina. I've said all I'm going to."

He turned away and moved into the forest. She sighed and followed him.

MACRINA WIPED HER FACE to get the water out of her eyes. She pushed at her tangled hair impatiently as they tramped through the dripping forest. It was raining. Again. Winter in this part of the Empire was mild, because the mountains were near the Black Sea, and so it was wet rather than snowy. Still, right now she would settle for some nice, crisp snow instead of the constant pattering rain. If they had a cave, or a hut made of evergreen branches, even, it would be better than this, she thought.

She was so sick of moving, of being dirty and tired. She knew she smelled. Basil and Mus reeked like garbage in the streets after a long hot spell. Nobody could go this long without a proper bath, without stinking like a rotting fish.

She longed for fresh faces and new voices. Oh, she loved Basil and Mus, but they were men, and her family. They didn't understand, the way Claudia did—or had done—about how she felt and what she thought.

Was Claudia even alive? Who was left, and were the persecutions letting up? It was impossible to know, tramping like this through the mud, shivering in the chill wind, never entering a village or seeing another face.

She sighed and brushed a tear from her eye. At home in this weather, she and Claudia would spend an afternoon with the braziers glowing, tucked under blankets and wraps, talking, laughing, and nibbling the wonderful tidbits cook made. Sometimes they would go to the baths and spend hours soaking in the hot water until the very centre of their bones warmed and their muscles felt loose and half-melted. They'd chat with each other and the other women who came to be warmed and cleaned.

She wondered, rubbing her wet, icy hands together, if she'd ever be that warm again.

Basil looked to the left and stopped.

"What?" asked Macrina.

"Just through there—is that a clearing?"

Macrina peered through the scrubby underbrush and trees. Even with the bare branches, there were enough evergreens that it was hard to see more than a few feet.

"It might be," she said, hugging herself. "It looks like it."

They pushed their way through the dripping brush. It was a clearing, and glory to God, there was a cave on one edge. She sprinted across the open space and stepped into the gloom.

A deep snarl froze her in place. She peered into the cave, eyes straining to see more than inky blackness. The low growl, heavy with threat, rumbled through her belly. Her heart thudded twice, heavily and hard, as though it were determined to burst out of her ribs, then settled to a rapid hard beat.

The sound of pebbles grating on rock, of fur and heavy muscle brushing stone in the deepest corner of the grotto rippled up her spine. The hairs at the back of her neck stood stiff and straight.

She drew back the tiniest fraction. Claws scraped stone in the dark, as the low threatening rumble intensified. It seemed made of the darkness, weaving around her like a spell, and she dared not move or it would envelop her.

"Let's see, let's see, Mama—is it as nice as our first one? Does it have—"

Without thinking, Macrina whirled and tackled her son. They smacked the bare, muddy earth. Four heavy, furred feet slammed onto her back, forcing her face into the mud. The heavy bass growl drove into her head and arrowed straight for her heart. She lunged up even as she gagged at the hot rotted breath whistling in her face. Though she pushed with all her strength, the fur-covered bulk barely moved. Beneath her Mus lay still and silent.

She snarled herself, pushing even harder, and lifting just enough to feel Mus's chest expand and hear his gasp of indrawn air.

The beast bore down, then leaped away, its claws slicing burning stripes across her shoulders and down her back.

In the next instant, Basil was over them, bow in one hand, hauling them up with the other, exclaiming over the wounds.

"Wolf," was all he said as he dragged them away from the clearing back into the forest.

Macrina didn't mind—she wanted to be miles from the source of that awful snarl, that hot and death-laden breath, those claws on her back.

Through bushes they crashed, Macrina heedless of her wounds or of the branches slapping across them. They ran across bare patches of ground, mud squelching and spattering her legs, cold and slimy. Thorns and brambles scraped her arms, her face, her legs, the wind whistled cold down her throat. Basil ran just ahead of her; Mus clung to him, ducking the branches as best he could.

She felt a burning wrench across the bones of her foot and she was down, the earth slamming against her cheek and palms, cold and wet, unforgiving and unyielding.

In a moment, Basil was beside her, lifting her. He set her on her feet and held her until her breath returned.

"All right?" Basil asked.

She shook her head. Her foot throbbed, the scratches stung, and her back was on fire. No, she wasn't all right. A harsh bitterness flooded through her so she could taste it—metallic, sour, and old.

"I'm hurt. I'm scared. I could have died! I want to stop.

I don't want to live in caves and be attacked by animals.

"I want to go home and be safe and clean and healed. I want a bath and I want to put on the perfume you bought me. I want a good meal cooked over a proper charcoal fire, by someone else, and I want to eat it in a proper dining room on a proper couch. I want to sleep in my own bed in my own house in my own city. I want to go to liturgy and vespers and say the prayers with my friends. I want to see Claudia and Flavius. I want to go home, Basil." Her voice broke on her husband's name and she covered her face with her hands. The tears leaked through her fingers.

Basil wrapped his arms around her, and stroked her hair, while Mus patted her arm.

"I'm sorry, my love," Basil whispered.

"It's not your fault, and I know it's God's will, but I'm so scared and tired and dirty."

"I know, I know," he said. "We'll try and find a good cave, and a secure hiding spot near a nice deep river where we can bathe. We'll learn how to tan hides and make clothing—"

"I don't want a safe cave and a deep river and a deer-hide tunic," she shouted. She pulled away from him, her fear and sorrow overlaid by anger. "I want my house and my baths and a wool tunic, and a silken *dalmatica*. I don't want to be chased and hounded like the hinds you hunt!" She raged and stamped her feet and hit a tree. It hurt, but felt good, so she did it again, and again. She kicked the trees and stamped the earth, she shrieked aloud and sobbed. Bark pattered from an oak tree as she punched it, and branches whipped her when she slapped them. Mus stood in rigid terror and Basil watched in shocked alarm as she raged around the bushes and through the undergrowth.

She sank, finally exhausted, to the forest floor, panting, still sobbing, blood trickling down her back. New cuts on her hands welled more blood, and her face was smeared where she'd wiped her tears. Her arms ached, her feet throbbed, and the sides of her hands were tender with bruises.

"Mama?" asked Mus, creeping up to her. He touched her gingerly on the arm. She reached out and ruffled his hair, then gathered him into a hug. Basil squatted down beside her and pulled them both into his arms, the wet and rain and mud making them a well-camouflaged trio.

"I'm sorry," she said when the sobs finally subsided.

Basil nodded and smoothed her hair away from her face. "You want to go home. So do I, my darling, but we can't. Not yet. Let me clean those wounds, and cover them with something." He took a deep breath and blew it out.

"Then we'll go on," Macrina said in a dull voice.

Chapter Four
Autumn 307

After they skirted a large town, the family found a small, dry cave.

Macrina hadn't bothered asking Basil to stop. He was right—it was too risky. People were greedy, and the empire paid well for Christians. If they were found out, all the years of hardship would be for nothing. God had looked after them so far, she thought bleakly. They were alive, and in reasonable health.

She would have to trust that if they were meant to

return home, He would let them know, but it was so hard. Even the obvious comforts of the cave and its dryness in the worst of the winter rains didn't help her sagging spirits.

MUS PLACED AN ACORN on the intersection of the lines Macrina had drawn in the dust.

"There! Four in a row. I win," he said with satisfaction.

"You always win at *merills*," she complained, but with a smile. "You're very good."

"Another game?" he asked.

She shook her head. "I have to lengthen your tunic. You're growing, and it's too short." She dug in the pack for a sewing needle, and tore a length of cloth from the end of Basil's old, worn toga.

She turned as Basil trudged into the clearing. His shoulders were stooped and he walked with a heavy, defeated tread.

Before they could speak, he ordered them to gather their things. Without protest, and with the ease of long practice, Macrina gathered the cooking utensils and jammed them into the pack, on top of the scriptures, letters, and relics. Mus gathered the few items scattered around the clearing. They doused the fire and set out again.

"I COULDN'T STAND TO SEE YOU so downcast and angry and upset," Basil explained after they stopped for the night. They were sitting in a space too small to be called a clearing; it was more a large gap between the trees, with only a few bushes crowding them.

The night was chilly but dry, and they didn't dare light a fire. Mus lay near them, wrapped in the remnants of the toga and palla, sound asleep. "I decided I'd risk it. This morning, while you were lighting the fire, I took the money from the pack, and instead of hunting, went into town to buy supplies and get news."

"But we'd traveled so far from it," she said.

Basil nodded. "When I was hunting, I found we'd actually gone round in circles—the town was less than half a day away.

"I got there just at noon and stopped to eat at the inn. It was busy, and I ended up sharing a table with a trader. Or I thought he was a trader. We got to talking. Partway through the conversation, he drew the fish on the table, in a drop of sauce."

Macrina nodded. It was still the secret signal—the *ichthus,* the fish shape.

"I drew a cross with the crust of my bread in the bowl of stew. He nodded to the street, so when we finished, I went out with him. He told me where a liturgy was starting at the sixth hour. I didn't think it would hurt to attend—it's been so long."

Macrina nodded sympathetically, suppressing the pang of envy and longing that sliced into her heart as she listened. "A liturgy—oh, Basil, of course! I'd have done the same—how could you not stay for it?"

He shrugged and went on. "I had some time, so I bought some tunics, and cleansing oil and a ***strigil***, thinking how much you'd like them, and how happy you'd be when I showed them to you. And I bought a pack to

33

carry the things back. I was late. I got to the house just as the soldiers did. The trader was with them, except he was no trader—he was a traitor, and a spy. He saw me and shouted, and they chased me. I was lucky to get away. But I lost the pack and everything in it."

Macrina's heart sank at the news. Not only to be moving again, but for Basil to have lost the new clothes! And there was no money left to replace them, either. At least she had her husband back, she told herself—that was most important. She pushed down her disappointment and worry and touched his arm. "Perhaps they didn't follow you."

Basil snorted. "They did—but I hope we can outrun them." He sighed and rubbed his hands through his hair. Next to her, Mus muttered in his sleep. She stroked her son's shoulder and he quieted.

"I'm sorry, Macrina," said Basil, finally.

"It's not your fault."

"If I'd not gone into town—"

"If I hadn't had that tantrum, you'd never have felt the need to take such a risk! Let it go, Basil. I moan and groan and complain about being dirty, and wanting to be clean and have perfume and a nice clean tunic. And you risk your life to get me those things. I don't deserve you, or Mus," she turned away from him, tears running down her cheeks. "If it hadn't been for me, we'd have the money and we'd be safe in the cave, not running again. Don't blame yourself. It's my fault, for being such a spoiled baby."

"Macrina, look at me," he took her by the shoulders and turned her to face him.

"If you hadn't had that tantrum, then I would never

34

have gone into town, and we'd have had no warning at all. If some of those Christians had escaped, the soldiers would have come searching and they would have found us."

"But why can't I be content? If God's caring for us, and looking out for us—and surely He must be, or we'd have died years ago—then why can't I just be grateful and happy with what He sends us? Why do I always want more?" She buried her face in his shoulder and sobbed. "All I want is to go home—I never think of the good things He's done for us, Basil, and I'm so selfish I send you into danger and risk all our lives, just because I want to be clean!"

She felt his hands on her back, rubbing and patting

her, trying to comfort her. After a few moments, she pulled back and wiped her eyes.

"We have been blessed—so very blessed. He's never let us be caught. We've always been able to get away. And this time, He's generous enough to let us get the news that it's not time yet to go home." She sighed and shook her head. "I have to learn to trust Him and wait on His time, not ours. But it's so hard."

Basil hugged her again. "I want to go home, too. But Macrina, it was my decision to go into town. You didn't force me. So don't take all the blame for yourself. I knew how risky it was, and I decided that I could be clever enough not to give myself away, and then I got taken in by the first man to show the right sign. We know there are spies and traitors—but fool that I was, I fell right into the trap, and almost got us caught and killed."

He stood and walked a little way into the night again. She could just make out his figure in the half-moonlight, leaning on an oak tree, his shoulders slumped. She should go and comfort him, she knew, but couldn't bring herself to get up and take the few necessary steps.

He wasn't ready to forgive himself—but neither was she ready to forgive herself. It was true, what she'd said—if she hadn't been so childish and selfish, and had a tantrum worthy of a nasty two-year-old, Basil would never have felt the need to go to town to buy her sweeties to make her happy. He could have been caught, and they'd never have seen him again. She sighed and curled on the ground, not far from Mus. She was just grateful that God was as forgiving and generous and merciful as He was, for she surely didn't deserve the benefits He kept sending them.

Chapter Five
Winter 308

B asil and Mus built a hut from deadfall, while Macrina tried her hand at fashioning shoes from tree bark. It worked about as well as the hut construction progressed, she thought. They had learned, over the years, to tan and treat animal skin so it didn't rot and stink, but hadn't yet learned the secret to making the soft, but tough leather of the shoes they'd known before their exile. Macrina wondered if tree bark might not be tougher and last longer, so she was trying it out.

The men were learning the secrets of the carpenters,

since there were no caves in the vicinity that were dry and deep enough for them.

"There. Hold it right there, Mus." Banging sounds. "Now, put it down and come see how we've done."

"Yes, Papa."

Macrina watched Mus closely as he moved to stand by his father. He'd grown again, she was sure. She moved up beside him and glanced out of the corner of her eyes. Sure enough—he was as tall as she was, now.

As she looked at the collection of limbs and branches that was to be their new home, the pile sighed and sagged, the green cedar fronds sliding off the back corner to the ground.

Basil stood for a moment, mouth open and shoulders sagging. "I was going to say, 'Welcome to your new home, **Domina,**' but it appears to need a bit more work."

Macrina bit back a smile, looked at Mus's disappointed face, and burst out laughing. "I'm sure it will be wonderful, when you finally get it to stay up," she said.

Basil glared at her for a moment, then laughed. "My training was in speechmaking and law, not carpentry," he said. "A woodsman would get a month's enjoyment from this. Come on, Mus, let's see what we've done wrong this time."

They eventually got it to stand, and to keep the rain off. When there was nothing else to do, Basil and Mus enjoyed their attempts to improve and enlarge the hut.

THE WEEKS PASSED PEACEFULLY ENOUGH. Basil and Mus hunted most days, staying close to camp only on days, like this one, when it was foggy and damp. Macrina could hear their voices outside.

"At your rebuke they fled: at the voice of your thunder they hastened away. They went up as high as the hills, and down to the valleys beneath," read Basil.

Mus repeated the verses as Macrina moved from the hut and sat between them, leaning against a large old log. The fog was so thick she couldn't see the rhododendrons on the other side of the clearing, about twenty steps away.

"Even unto the place which you had appointed for them. You set them their bounds which they should not pass, neither turn again to cover the earth," she finished.

"Tell a story, Mama," begged Mus.

Basil put the psalm pages back into the pack. "Please. We've done enough for now, and a story would be good."

Macrina thought, then brightened. "I know. I'll tell you a true story, about my spiritual father, Gregory."

"The first bishop of Neocaesarea?" asked Basil.

She nodded. "Yes. When he and his deacon turned to trees to hide from their pursuers. Do you know it?"

"No, tell me," demanded Mus. "I don't know it."

Macrina put her arm around him and gathered him close. He didn't fit into her lap anymore, but he made a comfortable, warm bundle by her side. She watched the tendrils of fog drift by as she thought.

"Well. This happened before I became a Christian, but some friends of mine were there, and they told me about it. It was during one of the persecutions, just after our governor had been appointed. I guess he felt he would make a good impression on Caesar if he got rid of all the Christians in his province."

"Was the persecution as bad as this one?" Mus asked.

"Oh, much worse," said Macrina. "It was awful. People were taken from their homes, from their work, and horrible things were done to them. It was as if they were in battle—children were taken and treated the same way as adults, women were treated even worse than men until they renounced their faith, and then they were killed in the most horrible and painful manner.

"Father Gregory, seeing that his people were in terrible fear, and knowing that the punishments were too strong for most of his flock, thought and prayed and wondered what to do. Every day, it seemed, there were more people missing, arrested and tortured. Most of those, it was rumored, were unable to stand up to the pain and recanted their faith. This caused Father Gregory much sorrow—he loved his children and he wanted them to have the fruits of their belief.

"So, after much thought and prayer, he decided that he had to tell his people to leave the city, and hide in the mountains."

"Like we're doing!" exclaimed Mus.

"Exactly like we're doing, but not for so long," agreed Macrina.

"Ohh," breathed Mus.

Basil glanced at Macrina and smiled. "It makes it better, knowing other people have done what we have?" he asked his son.

Mus shrugged, embarrassed. "It's as though—it's more—it feels more like a story," he tried to explain. "As though we're heroes in a tale instead of just us."

Macrina smiled. "I never thought of it like that before.

As though we're living a story that God is writing, to tell others who come after us what it's like to live for Him and suffer for Him."

Mus nodded.

"But how will people know about us?" asked Basil.

Mus shrugged. "God will tell them. And maybe we'll go back and tell people about what happened to us." He wiggled impatiently. "So tell the story, Mama."

"Well. Father Gregory had a deacon. This deacon used to be a priest of the temple to the pagan gods. When Father first came to Neocaesarea, he'd taken refuge in the temple during a storm, and had converted the man so well that he rarely left Gregory's side. And even though Gregory pleaded with him and all the Christians to flee, none of them would go, my friends said, until Gregory himself went with them.

"There were about fifty or sixty of them, and they traveled out of town until they came to a hill, with rocks and caverns and lots of places to hide."

"Were there trees?" asked Mus.

"Some, but not many. Do you remember the hill on the other side of Neocaesarea where we used to go and walk?"

Mus thought. "The one with all the red flowers in springtime? With the spring in the cave that made the waterfall we found that time?"

Macrina nodded. "That's the one."

"There aren't many trees there."

"No, there aren't. But Gregory took his people there. And the crowds who were persecuting them followed."

"It wasn't soldiers?"

Macrina shook her head. "It was mostly pagan towns-people who believed all kinds of awful things about Christians."

"Like what?"

"Oh, all kinds of things. That we eat all manner of filth and that we sacrifice people and drink their blood. Sheer nonsense and stupidity. But that's not part of this story.

"There were so many that they couldn't hide their trail, and it was easy for the pursuers to follow. The Christians hid in caverns and behind rocks. The other citizens surrounded the hill to make sure no one could escape, and they started to organize groups to send them up the hill.

"Now you have to understand how strong Gregory's faith was and how seriously he took his responsibility to his people. He knew that only God could save them all. The hill was surrounded and there were searchers everywhere, with torches and lanterns. They weren't going to leave the hill until they'd found every single Christian and dragged them all back to the city."

Chapter Six
Winter 308

"My friend told me that they were terrified, so frightened that most of them couldn't even pray. They were like little birds caught by a snake's stare."

Mus nodded, his eyes round and wide, mouth slightly open as he listened, riveted.

"Before they scattered to their hiding places, Father Gregory spoke to them. He recited from the Psalms, and from his talk they found the courage to scatter and hide, and pray. My friends hid in a rocky outcropping near

Father Gregory and the deacon, so Peter saw everything that happened."

"Bishop Peter?" asked Mus, voice cracking and eyes going even larger and wider than before.

Macrina nodded. "Yes, Bishop Peter. He wasn't a bishop or even a deacon then, though. He was very young, and he and Lydia had just married. He was the one who introduced me to Father Gregory."

"Oh," breathed Mus.

"The bishop stood a little way down the hill from where Peter and Lydia lay in the rocks. He stretched out his arms, and turned his head toward heaven. 'I will lift up mine eyes to the hills; from whence does my help come? My help comes from the Lord, who made heaven and earth. To Thee I lift up my eyes, O Thou who art enthroned in the heavens! Behold, as the eyes of servants look to the hand of their master, as the eyes of a maid to the hand of her mistress, we look to the Lord our God, till He have mercy on us.

"'Have mercy upon us, O Lord, have mercy upon us. If the Lord is not on our side, when men rise up against us, then they will have swallowed us up alive, when their anger is kindled against us.

"'Blessed be the Lord, who will not give us as prey to their teeth! Our help is in the name of the Lord, who made heaven and earth.'" Macrina shook her head. "Oh, I can't remember any more now, because he prayed and prayed and just didn't stop. At first, the people at the bottom of the hill were afraid to climb and start searching. They milled around on the level ground, talked in groups and walked around the hill—but none of them could find the courage to come up."

"Didn't they see Father Gregory?" Mus asked.

"They didn't appear to, Peter said. Certainly, no one pointed and shouted and charged up the hill to grab him. He just stood there praying. It gave the people courage to see that, Peter said.

"Finally, though, the persecutors began to move up the hill. Once one group started, the others set off for different parts of the hill, so no one could move from hiding spot to hiding spot.

"Some of them walked by Peter's hiding place, not more than twenty paces from where he and Lydia and one or two others huddled. One woman had a baby, Peter said, sound asleep in her arms. The searchers saw nothing! Peter used to talk about how his heart stopped because one man looked straight into his eyes!"

Mus gasped.

"But he looked away again, as if there was nothing and no one there. They searched the whole hill from the top, where that great craggy outcrop of rock stands so high—do you remember?"

Mus shook his head.

"I do," said Basil.

Macrina nodded. "From there all the way down to the very bottom, where their people stood guard, and back up again.

"Up the hill their leader stamped, furious and raging. He stopped not thirty paces from Father Gregory, who was still praying with his eyes on heaven.

"The leader stood with his hands on his hips, his toga rumpled and trailing on the ground. 'They have to behere!' he said. 'We followed them—fifty or sixty people, they left tracks as clear as a road. Where have they gone?

45

There's nothing here, nothing but rocks and a couple of trees'—and he pointed right at Father Gregory and the deacon."

Macrina laughed.

"What, Mama? What's so funny?"

"Father Gregory's deacon. He was a dear man, may his memory be eternal, but he had less faith than Father. But his courage was strong and abundant. He wouldn't leave Father, not even to hide, Peter said, but stood behind Gregory in plain sight, shaking and pale. When the leader came up from the bottom of the hill, he stood as still as he could, but Peter said he could see the sweat on the deacon's head—he was quite bald, you know—running down his skull. The deacon turned his head to watch the pagan leader, his eyes almost falling out of his head, he was so frightened. But he never moved—he stayed right beside Gregory the whole time.

"And all the leader saw were two trees on the side of an empty hill!"

Mus's eyes were wide and bright. He opened his mouth to say something but froze as a horse's whinny sounded—seemingly right next to them. He gripped Macrina's hand, squeezing her bones together in his terror, but he said not a word.

"Somewhere here," she heard a man call.

Macrina's heart sank—he'd heard her voice, and now it was just a matter of time. Slowly, she looked around, too frightened for even the simplest prayer.

She could hear a man's voice, the jingle of the harness and the stamp of a horse's hoof, as clearly as if they were beside her, but could see nothing but grey and white fog. She knew that in such weather, voices and sounds became distorted, and the fog played tricks with distance and clarity, but she was still too frightened to move.

She heard crashes and thumps, the sounds of feet stomping uncaring through bush, and a voice uttering what sounded from the tone like an oath.

"I heard a voice, very near here."

She turned her head. Basil looked into her eyes and shook his head.

"Stay," he mouthed. She nodded. If they couldn't see the searchers, the searchers couldn't see them—and any noise would only alert them to the fact they were close. She clung to Basil's hand and prayed.

Beside her, Mus shifted. His mouth was open, his face turned to the sky, arms rising from his sides. Before he could utter more than, "Oh Lord," Basil leaned over her

and hauled him down. Macrina slapped her hand over her fool son's mouth and glared at him. Only the fear of being located kept her from blistering his ears with her angry words. She sat and fumed, and quaked in fear, prayers forgotten as they waited.

The fog hung, white and blanketing. Between the searchers' voices and their noisy trampling, the only sound was the dripping of water from leaves and branches.

How long they sat, in terror and trust, hoping and breathless with fear, Macrina didn't know. But whether it was the fog, or God, or both, the searchers never seemed to stumble through the ring of trees and bushes onto the fugitives.

Finally, the noise died away, but they sat longer still, until the diffuse light began to fail, and darkness replaced the fog.

While Macrina prepared a cold meal, not daring to light a fire, Basil took Mus to the other side of the clearing. She heard her husband's intense, quiet voice for some time. Mus she heard scarcely at all—an occasional grunt, or "Yes, Papa," was all he said.

They packed up and moved the next morning. He had told Mus, Basil said as they walked, to think about wonders and miracles, and to think also about how much faith someone had to have before the name "Wonderworker" became attached to his own.

Macrina nodded, watching her son tramp listlessly ahead of them.

"I agree, Basil, he did put us at risk. But think about what he did."

"He nearly gave away our position to soldiers of the emperor, that's what he did!" Basil's voice rose, and ahead of them Mus winced and hunched his shoulders against his father's angry tone.

"Yes, and I was furious too. But I thought about it all last night. He had more faith than we did."

"He had more stupidity than we did!"

She paused and touched her husband's arm. "No." She glanced at Mus, speaking so he could hear. "We were afraid to trust that the Lord sent the fog and that He would protect us. Mus wasn't. He trusted that the Lord who loved Gregory enough to fool his enemies would love him, Mus, just as much and protect him just as thoroughly. Yes, he put us at risk, and yes, we were afraid of being arrested. Mus simply loved God and trusted Him to do the right thing. Can you fault him for learning the things we're teaching him, Basil?"

Basil scowled, grunted, and strode ahead, but he ruffled Mus's hair as he passed the boy. Macrina trudged behind, noting that her son's shoulders were straighter and he had a little more spring in his step.

The cave was dry and uninhabited, the clearing bright and sunny, and a stream bordered one side. There was no town within a day's walk; no charcoal burners or hunters ever came this way.

The floor of the cave was lumpier than their first one, the clearing smaller, and they had to dig out several thorny bushes, but Macrina had enjoyed the labor.

The stream flowed clear and clean. It wasn't as deep or as fast as the first one, so many years ago, only calf deep when they'd first arrived. Now, it was dry. Even the little puddles had disappeared. The rains hadn't come. The fog that had hidden them was the last moisture the family had felt. It had been bitterly cold, but even so, little snow fell.

Spring appeared, marked only by the lengthening days and warming air. Still no rain fell, and the plants that did survive were small. The blossoms on the bramble and blackberry bushes were few, with even fewer fruits.

As fall drew near, the days cooled off, and the morning chill meant a fire, Macrina began to think this would be their last home. If the drought didn't end, they would surely starve. The animals had migrated long ago, and there were precious few plants to eat.

She sat down by the cave mouth in the pale winter sun, too weak and tired to look for more greens or collect more deadfall for firewood. Although he'd gone again this morning, her Basil barely had strength to hunt.

Mus was skin over bone. He said little, and complained only when the hunger bit hardest.

In spite of the starvation, as weak as she was, Macrina still found life too sweet to want to leave it. I'd make a terrible martyr, she thought, tears trickling down her sunken cheeks. Please God, I don't want to die. I'm not ready yet.

"Sing Gladsome Light, Mama," begged her son.

"It's early, but if you sing it with me, I will," said Macrina. Their weak voices scarcely reached to the edge of the clearing. " . . . Heavenly, Holy, O Blessed Jesus Christ. Now that we have come to the setting of the sun . . ."

Basil staggered into the clearing, shoulders slumped and hands empty.

"I could hit nothing," he said, sitting heavily on a log near them.

"Never mind," said Macrina, climbing to her feet. "We found some greens. We'll eat those, and tomorrow you will bring down a lovely buck."

"Don't be so cheerful, Macrina," Basil said. "We're dying and it's my fault." He dropped his head into his hands and sat as still as a statue.

Macrina bowed to Basil as low as she could, her dull eyes lightened with a bit of mischief. "Ah—God has returned to us in the body! I want to have a word with you, my Lord, about this drought."

She wagged her finger at her husband as a smile threatened to break the seriousness of her expression. "And about the lack of water in the stream. And the shortage of greens and animals to hunt. Couldn't you arrange things a little better, and have only one shortage at time?"

Basil looked up from his hands, puzzled.

"At least," she continued, "that way we'd know whether to die of starvation or thirst. It's very inconsiderate of you, and very hard on us, to know which will serve your will better."

Basil smiled a little and took her hand. "Thank you, Macrina, but there is food out there. I can hear it, and sometimes I can see it, but I'm shaking too badly to hit it, the few times I do see something. If I were a better hunter—"

"If you were a better hunter, you'd have been a huntsman and would never have met and married me. And I wouldn't be here with you and would instead have died a martyr's death, which wouldn't have been nearly so good as having lived all these years with you." Her voice shook, not with emotion, but weakness. Even so, she put all the force she had into her words.

"You are not God, Basil, and He has worked this out as He wills, not as we would have it. I bless Him that I didn't die a martyr, for all that would guarantee me entry to heaven. The very thought makes my blood freeze, and I thank Him that I've had such a wise and caring Father, who will give me what I need—an exile in which I can love God, my husband, and my son.

"Now sit there. I meant it about the greens. About the hind—well, God will arrange for that or not, as He pleases."

Basil smiled and stroked her cheek with a thin hand as she gestured to Mus to bring the bowl half-filled with limp, bedraggled leaves and a few dried-out berries. They said the blessing, then shared out the last bit of food.

"If God is so good, why doesn't He send us real food?"

Mus complained. "If He loves us, why does He let us starve? Why does He let us suffer?"

"I can't read God's mind, Mus," the elder Basil replied. He tousled his son's hair gently. "Perhaps this is His way of telling Emperor Diocletian to let His people alone. Remember the things He did to the Egyptians, when Moses led His people out of bondage."

"But they were enemies, Papa. We're not. It's not fair."

"No, it doesn't seem fair, does it?" said Macrina, trying to convince herself as much as her son. "But we will have held the faith and been a witness for God. That's all that matters."

The wind rustling in the dry, limp leaves and the few remaining birds chirping in the distance were the only sounds as little Basil thought it over.

"I don't think I love God very much," he said finally, in a low voice.

Basil hugged him. "I know it's hard. But that is a Christian's job, my son. To love God and to trust Him, no matter how bad things are."

"Trust Him how?"

"Trust Him to love us infinitely," Macrina said. "Trust that His justice is the best for us no matter what. Trust enough to love Him when things are even this bad. Trust that we will be enfolded in His grace and mercy."

"Even if we die?"

"Especially if we die," said Macrina. "Because then we can go to heaven, and see Him and all the saints."

"It's hard, Mama. Do you always trust God like that?"

Macrina paused. An hour ago, she had prayed to live. She couldn't lie. "I try, but like you, I have questions. I don't want to die yet. I've been afraid when the soldiers have come close, or we've seen people who might hurt us."

"But you still trust God. You keep praying."

"Yes. It's all I can do. It's that or—"

Mus gasped, grabbed Macrina's arm and pointed to the edge of the clearing. In the evening's shadows stood a scrawny deer. Macrina and her son froze, barely daring to breathe or believe.

Moving slowly and cautiously, Basil stood and picked up his bow. He nocked an arrow, took a deep breath, held it, and let the arrow fly. It struck true, and the hind crumpled, dead.

Chapter Eight
Pascha 310

The sun wasn't shining. The cave was dim, but Macrina's body told her it was the normal time to waken—just after sunrise, when on a cloudless day the light poured into the cave and brightened it as though it were lit with a hundred lamps.

Macrina tensed but lay still. A cloudy day? No, she thought, the light wasn't right for clouds and overcast. She lay still, thinking and feeling, knowing that something was different, that somehow things had changed.

Beside her, Mus and Basil lay quietly, their breathing the breath of sleep, deep and even. She heard the birds singing their praises to God outside the cave.

What was it? Something blocking the cave entrance? Her heart sped up and sweat broke out on her palms.

She breathed in sour, acrid odors. Old sweat, dried blood, and leather. Something blocking the entrance, and the smell of sweat, blood, and leather. She closed her eyes. The soldiers had found them, finally. Her hands went cold and her breath stopped. *Oh God, let your will be done. And let us submit to it with good heart and courage,* she prayed. *But make it quick and painless, please, Father.*

As though he could hear her, the shape in the entrance said, "Christ is risen."

Shocked by the words, which were so out of joint with her imaginings, she sat up and replied without thinking. "Indeed, He is Risen. Is it Pascha?"

Beside her Basil stirred and went still again.

"Pascha was seven or eight days ago. I saw your fire pit and the cross over the entrance. I sometimes use this cave when I'm hunting. Will you share my catch?"

Macrina rubbed her eyes and shook her head. This must be a dream. Was she really sitting in bed, talking with a total stranger—a Christian stranger at that? She peered at him, but could make out nothing beyond a man-shape crouched in the doorway, bright morning light streaming by and glowing behind him—too bright to see his features or the details of his clothing.

She had spoken to no one but Basil and Mus for so long, it felt odd to speak to another human being. Yet the conventions dropped into place without thought, and she felt as though she were floating a little way above her own head.

"We'd be glad to, if you would share our meager meal."

THEY SAT AROUND THE FIRE, eating the rabbit Sevarius the hunter had supplied, the remains of the goat Basil had shot the day before, and greens Macrina had hastily gathered.

"Seven years?" Macrina stared at the hunter. "We've been in exile for seven years?"

Beside her, Basil choked. Macrina stared at him, too dumbfounded to move, and their new friend had to get up and pound her husband on the back.

"You're sure about this?" Basil said when he'd recovered. He was pale, and not just from the choking, Macrina thought. He looked as white as she felt.

The huntsman nodded. "From what you told me, you went into exile very early in the last great persecution, the one Diocletian and Maximian proclaimed. You were among the first victims. That means you'd been away two years when Diocletian and Maximian abdicated.

"Constantine and Maxentius took their places five years ago. They've been fighting with each other and everyone else who wants to rule ever since. Word is that Constantine is tolerant of us, but Maxentius is no friend to us Christians, so the persecution goes on when he's not off fighting somebody. People have more important things to worry about now the drought and famine is mostly over, and Governor Marcellus knows he'll have to at least tolerate us, especially if Constantine comes out victorious."

"Is this Constantine a Christian, then?" asked Basil.

Sevarius shrugged. "I've heard he's not, but I've also heard he's very sympathetic. And his mother, they say, is a devout Christian."

Macrina sat stunned. "I knew time had passed," she said quietly, musing aloud. "The seasons come and go, and we mark them and remember them as clearly as we can. But things blur, one winter into another, and it's hard to remember just how much time has gone by."

The hunter looked at her, amusement and sympathy in his face.

"Mus has grown, he's taller than me now, and his voice is changing. No wonder! He's thirteen." She turned toward the cave. "Mus, do you hear that? You're thirteen years old. No wonder you're so tall."

A whimper straggled out of the cave. Mus had refused to leave, had scrambled, terrified, behind Macrina and Basil once he woke and realized that a stranger was in their midst.

"Is he a soldier?" he'd whispered to Macrina. Basil picked up the conversation with the man as Macrina reached into the cave behind her and tried to pull her son around to her front.

His frantic struggles to back away persuaded her to stop. She contented herself with holding his hand as he cowered behind her just inside the entrance to the cave.

"No, he's no soldier, mousekin," she whispered. "He's just a man, out hunting for his family. He's Christian, like us. He won't hurt us."

Even so, Mus wouldn't stir when they moved into the brightening day. She'd taken him some rabbit and some of their goat for a breaking of the fast.

Now she sat, still stunned by the news, unable to absorb it.

She rocked back and dropped her rabbit thigh. The hunter's words echoed in her mind and their meaning burst on her like a rainstorm after a drought. "Governor Marcellus will have to tolerate us."

Tears soaked her cheeks and tunic as she sat, shaking from head to foot. She looked at Basil, a blurry shape on the other side of the fire.

"We can go home," she said.

Section Two
Homeless

Chapter Nine
Ascension 310

Bright lamplight spilled from the building into the street. The low babble of people arriving for the service reached Macrina and her family as they stood quietly in the shadows near the building.

Little Basil, still her Mus despite his thirteen years, clung to Macrina's hand in panic, drawing the little warmth that remained from her fingers, already icy with fear. How she had longed for this moment in their exile, to participate in the liturgy again, and now, how fearful she was!

She touched the reliquary with her foot where it rested on the pavement, as if Gregory's bones could protect her from the crowd of worshippers. So many, many people. She hadn't seen this many humans for so long. It was too much, too quickly. And how many would she know? She recognized no one who had passed or entered the church. How many were in exile or had been killed?

She turned away. From behind them, Basil laid a hand as cold as her own on her shoulder.

"They are our family," he said quietly.

"It's been seven years," she whispered.

"Yes, but they are family."

"How many are left?"

"We have to go in sooner or later, Macrina." He squeezed her shoulder and stroked her neck with a finger.

The younger Basil looked up at his father, face pale but for two bright flushes on his cheeks. "I'm scared."

"I know, son." Basil's voice was quiet and tender, with just a slight tremor in the low tones. "So am I." He pushed them gently forward, toward the light.

Macrina paused inside the doors. The room, built to hold over one hundred and fifty souls, was by no means crowded, yet the eighty or so who'd gathered here seemed like too many. Where was Claudia? And Flavius, and Marcellus, Antony and Egeria? So many new faces. She moved a step or two into the sanctuary, holding tight to Basil's hand. A woman standing next to the **ambo** on the women's side of the church turned, as if to see the size of the congregation. She looked familiar, thought Macrina. The alert, interested expression on her face, and that slight quirk to the left side of the mouth, as if she could see a delightful joke and wanted to share it, reminded Macrina of someone. It was achingly familiar, but she couldn't place it.

The woman's jaw dropped and her hands flew to her mouth. "Macrina?" she gasped. "Macrina!"

She flew across the room and flung her arms around Macrina, as the other worshippers turned, curious to see the newcomers.

"Claudia!" Macrina gasped and burst into tears. More lines on the face, more grief as well, but still her dearest friend. Praise God she'd lived. The women clung together, crying and laughing, while Basil greeted other Christians and sheltered his timid son.

Claudia drew Macrina's arm through her own. "Come, stand with me," she said.

Basil gestured with his chin. "Go, love. I'll give this—" he indicated the reliquary he cradled in both arms—"to Bishop Peter."

She moved toward the women's side, then looked back, a little panicky. Basil smiled and gestured to her to go on.

Mus whimpered and reached out to his mother as Basil moved with him to the men's side of the church. Macrina stretched her hand toward the boy and blew him a kiss.

She stood amid the other women, more relaxed at Claudia's closeness and reassuring familiarity.

"You remember Olivia, don't you?" Claudia asked, indicating a young woman with a child in her arms and another clinging to the edge of her bright blue palla. "Olivia, this is Macrina, returned from exile!"

"The last time I saw you, you were eleven!" Macrina said. "And look at you now. A matron and a mother."

Olivia smiled sadly and nodded to Macrina. "Forgive me, Domina," she said, "but I don't really remember you."

"No, I wouldn't expect you to," replied Macrina. "Your children are handsome."

Unexpectedly, the woman's eyes filled with tears, and she turned away with a mumbled, "Thank you, excuse me."

Claudia deftly steered Macrina away from the upset woman.

"She was arrested with her husband and saw his execution," Claudia whispered. "She also was tortured, but they let her go."

Before Macrina could say anything, an older woman approached.

"Claudia, who is your new friend?" she asked. Her silken dalmatica boasted a wide band of elaborate embroidery around the hem. Her palla, too, was silk, and of a delicate red, one of the most difficult dyes to obtain and therefore horrendously expensive. Only the richest wore it, and the way this woman twitched and adjusted the garment made it clear to Macrina that she wanted people to know how wealthy she was. Her hennaed hair, elaborately arranged, winked with rubies and emeralds.

"Selina, I'd like you to meet my dearest and oldest friend, Macrina."

The woman bowed deeply, too deeply for good manners. "The great and wonderful Macrina! You have no idea how much I've heard about you, my dear. Why, such hardship you've undergone! It couldn't have been worse if you'd been martyred. What a blessing that God is so generous to allow you to reap the benefit of such suffering here, with all your fame. And to have all your belongings and property still intact and waiting for you, that is a miracle. Still, I thought you'd look less—careworn, less—*plebeian*."

Macrina flushed. Selina's superior tone offended even more than her words. In church, in the family, social standing was not supposed to matter. Slave, freedwoman, or *patrician*, all were equal in the eyes of the Lord, and so should be equal in the church family. But it didn't always work that way, and some people were like Selina, overly concerned with who you were in the world.

"God saw fit to spare us," Macrina said stiffly. She fumed inside, and tightened her lips against the words that wanted to spill out. "It's not my place to question the Lord's decisions, only to be thankful for the mercies He gives us. We returned yesterday."

Clearly, this didn't sit well with Selina. "Oh, I see," she said. "My husband is consulting on Emperor Constantine's behalf with Governor Marcellus. We are quite close to the emperor. Welcome home. Claudia, I will see you after liturgy?" Claudia nodded as the woman turned and glided away.

"Who is she?" asked Macrina.

"Well, she is a Christian, so we should be charitable," Claudia whispered. She leaned even closer to Macrina and breathed in her ear, "But I'm afraid she's hard to love. I consider it a lesson in tolerance and patience."

Claudia pulled back and spoke in a more normal whisper. "She's been here about a year, and this is the first time she hasn't mentioned how provincial and backward everything is. But her husband is here on the emperor's behalf. Because of Flavius's position in the government, she's decided I'm worth talking to. Never mind. Just stand here and enjoy being home."

Breathing in the warm, incense-filled air, Macrina relaxed. The odor, the solid marble under her feet, and the rustle of clothing and quiet voices brought back memories of all the other liturgies she'd attended. Sanctity smelled like sandalwood, she thought, and smiled. She felt at home for the first time since they'd returned.

How good God was to keep us alive, and how blessed I am to participate in the liturgy again, she thought.

"Peace be unto all," intoned the bishop.

A thrill went through her as she heard her own voice mingling with those of the other members of her family, her true, real, and oh-so-loved family of faith, in the response: "And to your spirit."

Her eyes filled with tears and she cried for joy through the entire liturgy. The words washed over her and into her, soaking her soul in peace and exaltation.

She approached the priest as he held the bread and cup, her entire being yearning toward the morsel in his hands. She barely heard the words of the bishop, "The handmaiden of God Macrina . . ." She took the bread into her hands, and lifted the Body to her mouth. The gold chalice felt cool on her lips. As the blessed liquid entered her mouth, an electric thrill went through her, filling her with a warm, sweet light. She drifted back to her place, hardly aware of where she was or who she was with, so filled with joy and peace was she.

Chapter Ten
Pentecost 310

Macrina surveyed her dining room and sighed in deep satisfaction. Basil's brother had kept the house well while they were gone. All their belongings were safe, but the house had been unlived in for so long, it had been musty, damp, and chilly when they returned. Several days of burning braziers and concentrated sweeping and washing brought it back to a habitable comfort, and in no place more than the heart of the house—her dining room.

The polished wooden couches shone in the early evening light that streamed in through the window, and the low tables in front of them glowed with the servant's industry. Her ***mater's chair*** gave her a special joy, and she ran her arm along it as she moved into the room. Made of beautifully carved and finished citrus wood, it had no arms, and was her own special chair. No one else sat in it.

The house was hers again, and as she moved to the lamp in the centre of the room, she offered a quick, but heartfelt prayer of thanks to be home. As she lit the lamp, she sang the evening prayer, " . . . and behold the light of evening, we praise God: Father, Son and Holy Spir—"

The doors burst open and soldiers rushed in. The lamp dropped from Macrina's hand and smashed on the floor as she turned to flee. She slipped in the spilled oil. A soldier grabbed her. She jerked away, but his grip was too firm. He slapped her in the face, and cuffed her ear. Her head rang with the blow and her cheek stung and burned. Teeth clenched tight, Macrina grabbed the doorjamb as he dragged her toward the atrium. He cursed and pried her fingers away from the wall. Wild with fear, panting harshly, she closed her hand into a fist and punched his arm. He laughed, grabbed her arm and twisted. With a cry, she stumbled and almost fell, but he hauled her up and dragged her into a corner of the atrium.

She huddled there for a moment, terrified, then drew herself up. *I can't show them I'm afraid,* she thought, *even if they kill me right now. Oh good God, make it quick, make it very quick, and thank you that Mus is away at school!*

Her shoulders square, head held high, hands behind her tunic so the men wouldn't see them trembling, she watched the soldiers destroy her house. Their booted feet scarred the mosaic floor as they threw chairs over and knocked pottery and vases off their stands. Scrolls and books were tossed from hand to hand as they flipped through them, papyrus and vellum sheets fluttered in pieces to the floor. Bits of furniture slid across the tiles into the walls. Screams and curses filled the air as the household struggled against the invaders.

Her pose weakened as, across the room, Basil emerged from his office, dragged by three of the intruders. Macrina gasped as he grabbed a vase and smashed it against a soldier's side. Shards sprayed over the red wool and leather armor as they dragged him across the room.

He slammed into the wall beside her, clutching his toga, which trailed from his shoulder to the floor, stains blooming on its edges from the puddles of lamp oil. His short grey-black hair was disheveled, he had a cut over one eye and another on his cheek. He and Macrina clung together in the corner, defeated. They couldn't rescue the scriptures or the copied letters from the apostles and saints and escape with them as they had before. Glory to God that Gregory's relics were safely hidden.

Their servants huddled against the far wall, submitting dumbly to the chains. As they were locked into the manacles, their simple, cheap jewelry was torn from them, rings or a pair of earrings they had been given as rewards for good service, or had bought for themselves with the little bits of coin they acquired.

The *centurion* gestured at several of the soldiers. They shoved the slaves into a line and pushed them down the hall toward the front door.

"What are you doing?" demanded Basil. "Those are our servants."

"Where are you taking them?" snapped Macrina.

The centurion approached them, ignoring their

protests. He reached toward her, but Macrina jerked away. She was backed into the corner and had nowhere to go, but he nodded to a **munifex**—a private, who grabbed her arms and held her. She stood rock still, barely able to endure his touch as the centurion stripped off her emerald necklace and earrings. He even tore off her gold wedding ring. She swallowed hard, as her fear burned away in the face of her anger. *They'd even take my wedding ring! What kind of pigs are they*, she thought, fuming. She clenched her teeth to keep her words behind her lips, and balled her fists, her nails dug deep into her palms. *I must stay calm. I cannot lose my temper*, she told herself.

After handing the jewelry to an aide, the centurion turned to face them.

Tunic torn, a bruise on one eye and her thick black hair half fallen over her shoulder and back, Macrina held herself stiffly erect. She stared straight into his eyes, daring him to do his worst.

The **tribune**, a large, red-faced man who had stood in the entry hall through the entire raid, moved in front of them and read from the scroll in his hands.

"Basil Marcellus Marius and Macrina Prima Severius. By order of the emperor, everything you own is forfeit. This house, your estates at Annesi, all your possessions belong now to the emperor." He looked up at them, sneering at their rumpled, bloody appearance. "The emperor is merciful. You may keep your lives and the clothes you are wearing."

He looked up at them. "And be sure, you are known. The governor, in the name of the emperor, will be watching you. Now get out."

As quickly as it had come, her anger drained away at

this last proclamation. She had expected to be arrested and taken to jail. But this—what was this?

The soldiers pushed them out of the house into a jeering crowd. Macrina and Basil clung together, bewildered and confused at the sudden turn of events. Rotten fruit rained down on them. A slimy lettuce hit her in the shoulder, and Basil cried out as a stone cut his ear. Intent only on escape, paying no attention to direction or corners, they ran into the cold spring twilight.

Some of the mob followed them for a time, hurling more rotten vegetables and fruit and a few stones after them.

They stopped running only when they reached the river, on the outskirts of town.

She knelt by the water's edge, sobbing as she scrubbed the slimy mess off her skin and tunic.

"We just got back!" she exclaimed. "How can they do this to us? Won't it ever stop?" She picked up a stone and threw it into the water, then collapsed on the bank, arms around her knees, shivering in the night air.

Basil climbed down the bank to sit beside her. He put his arm around her shoulders. "They can't get away with this," he said. "I'll send a message to Flavius in the morning. I'll talk to the bishop."

"Where are we going to sleep tonight?" she asked plaintively. She glanced at the sky. It was late dusk, almost dark now. She peered at Basil's injured ear, but it was too dark to see anything clearly. He patted her hand.

"It's fine, it didn't break the skin," he said. "I don't know, Macrina." His shoulders slumped and he plucked at the grass. "I thought things would be better with that edict."

"The Augustus hates us and so does the governor. He'll push as hard as he can without actually breaking the law. How Flavius has managed to keep his secret all these years, when he's so close to Marcellus, I don't know. Do you think Bishop Peter would take us in, at least for the night?"

"We can't ask him," said Basil. "It's too dangerous. You heard the tribune. We're marked. We'll lead the authorities right to anyone we stay with."

"And they'll be arrested and thrown out of their homes, or worse. Why is this happening to us?" wailed Macrina. She listened to her own words and then shook her head, laughing a little, through her tears. "I sound like Mus, back in the forest. I'm so glad he's in Caesarea with your brother."

Basil smiled sadly. "The school isn't as good as one in Athens, but at least he's where the government is sympathetic." He sighed and rubbed his hands over his head. "I have some money, we'll stay at an inn for tonight. I'll see the bishop first thing in the morning and start working to get our property back."

"They wouldn't even let me have my palla, Basil," she whispered, her voice trembling with reaction. "It's all gone. They even took my wedding band."

Basil gathered her in his arms and rocked her like a child. "It will be all right," he soothed. "God is still looking after us. We have to trust in Him, my love."

"I know," she said as she sat up and wiped the tears from her cheeks. "It's just so sudden. And Basil—we lost the scriptures and Saint Paul's letters that you were copying for the church. They destroyed all of them, I'm sure of it." She burst into tears again.

"It's a loss, I can't pretend it's not." He sighed heavily. "But I'm sure there will be other copies we can get. I'll talk to the bishop about that tomorrow, too. But we should get indoors. It's cold and looks like rain."

They looked up at the black night sky. No stars or moon showed in the inky darkness.

Basil rose to his feet. He gave her a hand up. In the thickening gloom, she could barely see his teeth as his lips parted in a smile. "Share the warmth of my toga?" he asked.

Her voice was shaky with emotion still, but she tried to seem brave. Smiling a little, she tucked her hand under his arm. "I would consider it an honor to share your toga, sir."

Chapter Eleven
Pentecost 310

acrina sat in the shade, her back against the wall of a fabric shop, and sighed with relief. She'd been wandering most of the day, hunger growing in her and desperation fueling her. Had it really been only days since they'd lost their home? It felt like weeks, months even.

She looked up and down the street, wondering if they would live the rest of their lives as destitute beggars.

The road was crowded with people and carts. Rich citizens strolled along the raised stone sidewalks, eating

79

and gossiping as they moved in and out of the ground-level stores. Macrina watched with amusement as a woman leaned out of an *insula* window above the store across the street and called to someone on the road. No one responded, and after a moment, the woman tossed something to the street below. It hit a man who was talking to a child. Annoyed, he turned, looked up, and smiled as the woman gestured to his feet. He picked it up, whatever it was, saluted her, and walked off with his son.

Messengers darted through the crowds, and slaves bore loads destined for the stores and homes. The rumbling of the carts from the surrounding countryside added to the cacophony as they trundled along the cobblestone roadway, bringing produce and goods into town for sale.

The smells of the city wafted over her—dung from the horses and donkeys, perfume from the shop across the street, hot stone, and always the smell of people, some clean, some not, some wearing enough scent to stun the nose at fifty paces, and some who had obviously not seen the inside of a bathhouse for far too long.

She caught a whiff of lamb and chicken sizzling on grills down the street. Macrina would have to find a way to get some food. There wouldn't be a liturgy for another few days, which meant that she couldn't count on a solid meal until then. Maybe a liturgy would make her feel better; it usually improved her mood.

Basil was meeting with the bishop again, still trying to get their property back. She wasn't needed at the meeting, and didn't really want to listen to the men talk, so she wandered through the city on this first truly warm summer day.

She nodded to one or two of her friends. Most of them

were as rich as she had been. She wouldn't embarrass them by speaking to them in the street—it would look bad, a poor freedwoman approaching a rich patrician. People might think she was begging. The very thought made her cheeks hot.

She spotted Selina staring at her from the perfume seller's shop across the street. Macrina nodded. Selina pointedly turned her back and addressed the slave standing next to her, handing her something. The woman crossed the street and dropped a coin at Macrina's knees.

"From my mistress. She says she hopes it will help you."

Macrina looked up, straight into Selina's narrowed eyes and superior smirk. Selina bowed gracefully before she turned back to the perfume vendor's wares.

The nerve of the woman! Macrina thought. *How dare she! I'm no beggar!*

She looked away, down the street, eyes bright with tears of shame, cheeks on fire. She caught a youth, about eleven, staring at her. He looked a bit like Mus at that age, she thought, but taller. The thought calmed her and she blinked away the tears.

He strolled over, his white tunic with a geometric red border bright in the sunshine. His shoes looked new and of good quality. Not a slave or a poor freedman's son. This was a child of wealth, a patrician's son.

"You're begging." The sneer evident in his voice as well as on his face put Macrina's teeth on edge. "I'm not," she exclaimed. "I'm simply sitting. I've been walking and my feet are tired."

"Huh. I don't believe you. What about the coin on the ground?"

Macrina shrugged. "I dropped it." So saying, she picked it up and tucked it away.

"I saw the slave give it to you. And if you're not begging, then what do you do? If you can, tell me a story, and I might give you a *sestertius.*"

"I can tell stories wonderfully, but I don't need your money, thank you."

"So tell me one anyway. I'm bored."

"I don't tell stories to rude children. They have to ask properly."

"My father says that beggars should be whipped and thrown out of the city, that's what my father says. And if you're rude to me again, I'll tell him and you will be beaten."

"Your father is—" she stopped, suddenly aware that this unpleasant child was her superior now. As long as she was homeless, moneyless, and wearing only her tunic, anything he said about her would be taken as fact, and anything she said in her own defense would be taken as lies. She swallowed her pride and said, through a smile that wished boiling water in his lap, "—undoubtedly a wise and important man."

The boy crossed his arms on his chest. "Tell me a story. And it better be good."

She inhaled and called upon all her patience. "Have you ever heard of the Wonderworker?"

The boy's brow furrowed and he cocked his head to one side. "The wonderworker? Who is that? One of the gods?"

Macrina shook her head and smoothed her tunic.

"No, he was a lawyer but he loved God, and he performed miracles. He lived here in Neocaesarea, you know."

"What sort of miracles? And when did he live here?"

"He lived a fair time ago—many years before you were born. He stopped two brothers from starting a war."

"What else?"

"Oh, he moved huge boulders, and drove demons out. He moved a river once, and turned himself and his disciple into trees when enemies were after him."

"Wait here. I'll get my brothers. These sound like good stories and I've never heard any of them before." He started off, then turned back and pointed at her. "Don't go away. Be here when I get back." He sprinted a few feet, then stopped once again. "And don't start telling until I return with my brothers."

What an obnoxious child! Even if he looked like Mus, her son would never speak to another like that, not even a servant. And the young man had brothers, who were probably worse than he. But it would keep her out of trouble, and she missed telling her stories to Mus.

She sighed and wondered how he was doing. The bishop would make sure word got to him down in Caesarea of what had happened, and that Mus was to stay with his uncle until they could find a way to join him or regain their possessions. But she missed him so much.

Two of the boys were quarreling as the gaggle approached. One pushed the other and was shoved in his turn, before the servant with them could separate them. The group gathered before her, and the obnoxious one nodded regally.

"During the reign of Decius," she began, "there lived in this city two brothers, the only sons of a very rich man.

This man owned a great amount of land. On one of the pieces of this man's property was a lake. It was large and clear and deep. Trees were scattered around it, and sandy beaches lined its edge. Rushes grew along the banks, and it was full of ducks and geese, fish and clams. Both boys loved the lake. They fished in it, hunted the birds and animals that lived near it, and swam and boated on it. All through their growing up, and even after they received their adult togas, they spent as much time as they could at the lake.

"Because they were personable and polite young men" (she glanced at Obnoxious), "they were both very popular fellows, and became even more popular when they brought their friends to enjoy the lake with them. But as popular as they were, they did quarrel, as brothers do, and more so when their father, who grew old in his years, sickened and died.

"Now because he knew they quarreled bitterly, the old man had decreed that his property be divided equally between the two brothers, with one exception. They were to share the lake. They were to learn to get along by sharing this property.

"The elder son, one Gaius by name, was exceedingly angry about this. He thought that because he was the elder, he should have gotten the lake. So he went to his brother.

"'Now we both know,' Gaius said, 'that of the two of us, father loved me best, and he always intended to leave the lake to me. It was just that stupid clerk who mixed up the division. So why don't I trade you two of my parcels of land for your share, and that way you'll have the best of the deal. And I'll tell you too, I'll let you come to the lake and use it whenever you want. You may swim and hunt, boat and fish on it, just as if it were your own.'"

"That sounds like a good proposal," said an older boy, obviously Obnoxious's elder brother. They shared the same hooked nose, firm chin, and superior expression. From the way he twitched his toga and adjusted his fine white linen tunic, Macrina guessed that he was about seventeen. He would have just received his tunic and his toga, the Roman marks of manhood and citizenship.

Some of the other boys nodded. "I'd take it in a minute," said one.

"Mmm—I don't know," said another. "How do you know the brother would keep his word? Maybe you'd sell it to him and then he'd say you couldn't use it." As if familiar with a brother's double dealing, he glanced at the boy next to him.

"But you'd still have two parcels of land instead of one," said Obnoxious. "I'd like that better than some stupid old lake that you couldn't farm or mine."

"I don't know," said one of the older boys, slowly. "I think I'd want the lake, if I loved it so much, and I'd had such fun there, fishing and swimming and hunting. I don't think I'd trade."

"Did they?" Obnoxious's brother asked. "What happened?"

Chapter Twelve
Pentecost 310

"Well," said Macrina, shifting position and wishing for a drink of juice, "the younger brother, whose name was Julius, refused. He loved the land just as much as his brother did. And he was hurt and angry that Gaius had claimed their father loved him better than Julius himself.

"The older brother made another offer. But Julius turned that one down as well.

"Back and forth they went, Gaius making offer after offer, and Julius refusing every one. The truth was that while each one badly wanted the lake, they equally badly *didn't* want the other to have it.

"Finally, Gaius stormed out and went straight to the law. The clerk decided that the matter should be put before the wise men of the city.

"The argument went all the way to the governor, they were so adamant in their positions. And the governor decreed that the two young men would share the lake, just as their father had wanted. Neither could trade it to the other, but they would, he said, have to learn to live in harmony and peace.

"Well! He might as well have ordered the rain to fall up and the fish to ride horses!"

She surveyed the crowd. It had grown as she'd talked, and there were several adults, as engrossed as the children. She noticed Selina at the edge of the crowd, accompanied by the deacon.

"Finally, Gaius decided to take the land by force. He made a plan to attack his brother's villa. He gathered all his friends, who talked to all their friends, who in turn talked to all their friends. At the end of all the talking, he had quite an army.

"Julius wasn't sitting still counting his grapes. He also gathered his friends and their friends, and ended up with an equally large army.

"The battle date was set, and the place—the lake itself—was set, too.

"Everyone in the city knew about the dispute, and they knew, too, about the governor's decision. The argument and the coming battle were the talk of the city for some weeks. Finally, someone thought to approach a learned man famous for his wisdom.

"Gregory was a wise and able man who performed great wonders. He was born here and went away to school, where he learned many important things. When he came back home, he practiced law and excelled at it. Many men in the city came to him and asked him to solve difficult problems and sort out questions of law and of business.

"The wise men of the city came to Gregory and explained the problem. Because of all the talk, he knew the story already and agreed to intervene. The night before the brothers' armies were to do battle, he went to the lake, and stayed in vigil all night long.

"He heard the two brothers' armies arrive. He heard them make camp on opposite sides of the lake. He listened to the insults the young men threw back and forth as they worked up their courage and blood-lust.

"'Ah,' thought Gregory to himself, 'they are eager to fight and kill each other. But they don't consider that they themselves might die, or what it feels like to have the death of another on their hands.

"'Oh good Lord,' he prayed, 'who rebuked Your disciple for taking arms against Your enemies when they arrested You, and who, although You commanded the power of the universe, allowed men to torture and kill You, allow me to glorify Your name and power by finding a solution for these brothers who would incite their friends to slaughter. Help me to teach them, O Lord, that Your might and power are greater than any man's, and that only by living by Your word can they obtain their hearts' true desires.'

"He prayed until the stars slept and the moon set. As the sun lightened the sky, the armies rose. The air filled with the clash of metal as they put on their armor and checked their weapons. The dust rose from the ground in clouds as they drew up into their formations."

"Who was he praying to? Mars?" asked Obnoxious.

"Mars is the god of war, empty-headed boy," said an adult. "Be still and let us listen."

Macrina paused and surveyed her audience. A sudden gleam on her right, back behind the crowd, caught her eye, and she peered toward it. She went cold all over as she recognized that the flash came from sunlight reflecting off armor.

She mastered her fear and faced her rapt audience. It was too late now, and she had to finish the story.

"Before the armies could approach one another, the sentries alerted the brothers. They pointed to Gregory, and everyone watched as he paced the edge of the lake, touching his staff in the water. Three times he circled the lake. He spoke to no one. He ignored the sentry's challenge and the brothers' questions about what he was doing."

"Why didn't they throw him off the land?" asked one of her listeners.

"Or kill him," added Obnoxious.

"Stupid child, he was obviously a citizen—you don't just kill a citizen." This was from someone who stood behind the brothers.

Macrina glanced to the back of the crowd. The soldier was still there, listening quietly. She nodded to the adult who'd made the comment. "That's true, but that's not why they left him alone. He was famous in the city. Everyone knew him for the miracles he'd performed and for the wisdom he showed. They didn't dare touch him or harm him, but instead, all the young men in both armies waited. They watched him and listened to him pray. They wondered if perhaps he would perform another of his miracles.

"Some said that he would split the lake in two, so that each brother could have his own lake. Others speculated that he would kill both men, and the land would go to someone else. And still others wondered if perhaps he would transport the armies far away, so that by the time they made their way back home, they would be old men and no longer interested in fighting.

"But he did none of those things. He walked up to the very edge of the water and struck the lake three times with his staff." Macrina paused. Her audience stared at her, enrapt. She gazed slowly around the crowd, meeting each person's eyes in turn. She nerved herself to stare at the soldier. He stared back, his expression neither as enrapt as the others, nor angry, nor cold. It gave away nothing. She shivered and moved her gaze, letting the silence stretch out until she'd mastered her fear, and letting the audience's tension build.

"The lake, on the third stroke of his staff—" She paused and the inhalation of the crowd was audible.

"—disappeared!"

They gasped.

"In its place was a huge meadow—grass grew on it, and bushes and flowers. Everyone was amazed and shocked by such a thing. But there was no reason to fight now, since there was no lake to fight over, so the brothers disbanded their armies and went home. They were so angry at Gregory for making the lake disappear that they quite forgot they'd been furious enough to kill each other. For the rest of their lives they got along quite well, finding a common cause in being angry at Gregory."

There was laughter and chatter as the crowd dispersed.

"That was a good story," said a little child, holding a slave's hand.

"Thank you," she replied. She caught a whiff of cardamom and cinnamon from the spice shop next to where she sat. It mingled with the scent of lamb grilling in olive oil and oregano at a stall down the street and made her stomach gurgle. She looked down and was surprised at the pile of coins by her knees. She hadn't intended to earn money by telling the story—it was simply to avoid trouble. But God had blessed her doubly! She'd told people about God's power, and now she had money to spend—on food, perhaps, or a room at an inn for the night.

She gathered up the coins, but paused when a pair of *caliga*-shod feet stopped in front of her. She looked up, her hands automatically plucking the last of the **tremis** from the ground, then rose, trembling with fear.

Chapter Thirteen
Pentecost 310

"It was a good story," the soldier said.

"Thank you," she replied, as calmly as she could. The clink of the coins as she pretended to count them covered the tremble in her voice—at least she hoped it did.

"It concerned the Christian God, didn't it?"

Macrina inhaled and nodded, peering at the metal in her hands with what she prayed looked like great absorption. *Why doesn't he just go away? Or arrest me for something*, she thought. He'd been listening for most of the story—and he was a soldier of the emperor. *He can't want anything good.*

"Twenty, twenty-one . . ."

"It's only eleven," he said gently, and covered her hands with his own. "I could take you to the temple, and see if you would burn the incense. But I know you wouldn't, and then I could arrest you." His voice was mild, neutral and quiet. She glanced up into his face, but it gave no indication of his thoughts or his feelings.

Anger bloomed in her. She was tired of this! He played her as her cats had played with the mice they caught—if he was going to arrest her, then let him do it! At least her uncertainty would be over.

She stuffed the coins away, looked into his face, and said quietly, but firmly, "'Right dear in His sight is the death of His saints.' If you want to arrest me on some false pretext, then do so, and the governor will be pleased and you will earn favor and perhaps a promotion. That will last until the next soldier distinguishes himself and you are forgotten.

"But if I am put to death, I will win the crown of a martyr and be in heaven with my Lord forever, and through my sacrifice God will win even more souls to Himself.

"So arrest me, soldier, or leave me alone." She brushed past him, but he grabbed her arm. She stared down at his hand as if it were some loathsome insect and then up into his face. "I am a Roman citizen. Get your hand off me." She yanked at it but couldn't free herself. She felt the blood leave her face. A lump formed in her throat as she stared at the man.

"Perhaps I should arrest you," he said in a mild voice.

Courage flowed into Macrina—leaving no room for anger and fear. She felt the color coming back to her face and her trembling ceased. Calmly, she looked him in the eye.

"'The Lord has searched you out and known you,'" she said. "'He knows your down-sitting and your uprising. He formed your inner parts, and knitted you together in your mother's womb.' He will have you one day. He died and rose for you as well as for me."

The man's face went white and his grip on her arm slackened.

"How did you know?" he whispered.

"Know what?" she asked. "I just quoted the Psalms. It's true, though. God has known you since before you were born. He has counted every hair on your head."

"I've been thinking—wondering about your beliefs. Where do you all get the courage? Do you know what we do to your people?"

She nodded and looked away. How could she not know? Word circulated, stories were told by some like Olivia, who for God's own reasons were released, about what they and the others had suffered. She had watched friends die, seen others released without eyes or hands or feet.

"Is it worth it?" he asked. "You're a woman of quality, I can see that in your attitude and the way you carry yourself. But here you are, telling stories to earn money and wearing a cast-off tunic and no shoes. What can be so important that you would risk everything you own, that you would risk torture and death for it?"

She smiled at him. "God's love."

He shook his head, baffled. "How can it be worth dying for?"

"If you give your life to God, if you acknowledge that Jesus the Christ lived and died and was raised from the dead so that you might have eternal life, then you will have eternal life. If you face a life of paradise, of being one with Love and with the God who created the universe and everything in it, who loved you enough to take your sins upon Himself, then what does the death of the flesh matter? You will go on, and you will survive, even if you are killed by unbelievers and God-haters."

"How does this happen?"

Macrina shook her head. "Not here and not now. It will take much more time than I have. What is your name?"

"Godarius. When can we talk, then?"

"We can meet here tomorrow afternoon. You come, in your tunic. No uniform, no weapons, no comrades. Either I or someone I send will meet you and talk with you about the faith then."

"You don't trust me?"

She laughed, a humorless, bitter sound. "You're a soldier. Your kind exiled me for seven years. Your kind tortured and killed the husband of a young woman with two tiny children. Would you trust a soldier if you were in my position?"

He shook his head slowly. "You're right. I wouldn't. Tomorrow, here, just after noon?"

She nodded. "Someone will come. It may not be me."

He bowed and walked away.

Macrina blew a gusty breath and fell back against the wall. She was shaking all over, and sweat beaded on her forehead and her neck and shoulders. She hoped she'd done the right thing. Well, they'd see tomorrow.

People flowed around her, the streets crowded and bright with sunlight. She heard a donkey bawling, a vendor crying his wares, children yelling. A juggler stood in the intersection, pretending to be utterly awful at his trade, and people laughed at his clumsiness.

The odor of the lamb wafted by her again, reminding her forcefully that she hadn't eaten since early the previous day. She could, and would, remedy that right now.

Just as she pushed herself away from the wall, Selina and the deacon approached her.

"Macrina, would you come with us, please?" Selina said. She and the deacon were serious, even grim. Their mouths were set in straight lines and they held themselves stiffly.

She looked from one to the other. "What's wrong? Is it Basil? Has something happened to Basil?"

"The bishop needs to see you, right away."

Her cheeks went cold and she gasped, hunger forgotten as dread settled on her shoulders. "It is, isn't it? Please, tell me what's happened to him?" Even as she asked the question, she strode away, ahead of them. They hurried to catch up, and flanked her as she trotted along the street.

"It's not Basil. He's fine," the deacon said. He cast a glance at Selina that Macrina couldn't interpret. Worry? Entreaty? Why was he worried? Why would he silently plead with this woman? The deacon was a leader in the church—he should be the one to issue the instructions, not Selina.

"What's going on?" Macrina asked him.

"You just never mind," answered Selina, every inch

the imperious patrician. "You'll find out when we get to the bishop's."

Macrina glanced at the deacon again, more confused and worried than ever. Had something happened to Basil? Or—she gasped and hurried along even more quickly— had they received news about her son? Had something happened to Mus? Was he ill? Hurt? Had he, against all assurances of sympathy in Caesarea, been arrested? She strode ahead, her companions scurrying to keep up.

"**M**acrina!" Basil exclaimed as they entered the bishop's atrium. He strode over to her.

"What—" she began.

"We must see the bishop at once, the matter is most urgent," said Selina icily, riding over Macrina.

"Macrina?" Basil asked, looking as puzzled as she felt.

She shrugged and shook her head. Peter, the bishop, joined them in the atrium, grasping Macrina's hands and greeting her warmly. He was only about ten years older than Macrina and had known her and her family for most of their lives, and shared her reverence for Gregory the Wonderworker.

"Bishop Peter, you won't be as friendly when you hear what I have to say," stated Selina. "This woman that you trust so much and hold in such high esteem, this woman —this *married* woman—is an adulteress! I heard her agreeing to meet a soldier, tonight, in the street!"

The room was silent with shock for a moment, then Macrina burst out laughing, so relieved was she that no disaster awaited her. Basil looked at his wife in surprise, then joined her hilarity.

"This is a serious charge, Selina," Peter said gravely, although his mouth twitched suspiciously. "Can you substantiate it?"

"The deacon heard it too," she said. "Didn't you, Simeon?"

"I, ahh, that is to say," he stammered, before Macrina interrupted him.

"He wanted to talk about the faith, Selina. I didn't trust him. If you had been listening as carefully as you say, you would have heard. I said tomorrow afternoon, not tonight. My exact words were: 'Someone will come. It may not be me.' That doesn't sound as though I were meeting him to commit adultery."

"Humph. A fine story."

"But it's true, Domina," said Simeon. "We heard it with our own ears."

"I don't know what you heard. I didn't hear all the conversation, I admit. But I did hear a woman agreeing to meet a man—a soldier, no less—after dark, and alone. That sounds like nothing honest." She paused, and then looked surprised, as if something had just occurred to her. "Or perhaps you were doing more than that. Perhaps you were agreeing to give him names, as well. You're not only an adulteress, you're a traitor to the faith! Did you tell him about Flavius? About Peter? Whom did you sell to the empire, Macrina?"

"You are wrong," declared Macrina, rage racing through her. Her face grew hot, and she clenched her fists. Her head lifted and she straightened her shoulders as she glared at Selina. "I've been a faithful Christian for years. I spent seven years in exile, and I've just been thrown out of my home. We've lost everything, even my wedding rings were taken. My parents disowned me because of my faith. My uncle was tortured and killed. My cousin died when she was twelve because of them. My best friend's first husband was killed in front of her eyes.

"I would no more betray my brothers and sisters than I could sprout wings and fly."

She took a step toward the insufferable woman, her voice rising and trembling. "Have you ever had to suffer for the faith? Or are you so safe with the emperor that no one will touch you for fear of him?"

Selina drew back her hand and slapped Macrina across the face. "You are nothing. You're a freedwoman and a plebeian, nothing more. You will not speak to me that way and you will address me as Domina. And I say you were committing adultery and selling names to the empire."

"My dear daughter—" began the bishop.

"Don't you call me a freedwoman, and don't you ever slap me again," said Macrina through gritted teeth, speaking over the bishop's words. "I am as patrician as you, my family have been patrician since before the republic, and no one can take that away from me, no matter how poor

I am. I've lost everything because I refuse to abandon my faith. Can you say the same? Have you ever lost anyone or anything because you had to make that choice?"

Selina spat at Macrina. "You may be patrician by birth, but you neither act it nor look it. You're nothing but a posturing, pious would-be saint. Oh, yes, Saint Macrina—wouldn't that make you glow! Well, that's what they call you behind your back. But they call you 'Saint Macrina to whom all must bow because she was exiled for seven years.'

"If you were really as pious as you'd like us to believe, you'd have died a martyr like all the rest who've perished for the faith. Huh! But not you! You'd rather prattle on about your exile and be comfortable!" Selina snarled. She turned on the bishop and wrenched her arm from his gentle grasp. "And don't you 'dear daughter' me! What are you going to do about her?"

"Why are you doing this, Domina?" asked the deacon. "Are you possessed of an evil spirit that you accuse one of our most stalwart members? I cannot believe what you say of Macrina. Yes, I heard her, but she said she might not meet the man, although someone would. And betraying us? No, I cannot believe this of our Macrina. Surely not."

Selina glared at them, her eyes glittering with hatred. "I see. I see. Well, if you won't believe me, I'll take this to Constantine. My husband is high in his regard, and we'll see what happens. We'll just see."

She whirled and stalked out of the house.

Macrina turned to Peter, Selina's accusations and wild talk burning in her ears and heart. "A pious posturer— I'm not! I scarcely talk about what happened. I've never thought of being a saint. God spared us for His own reasons—I've never questioned why. Do people really think that of me?"

The bishop patted her shoulder. "Do not worry. None of what she said was true, Macrina. She is jealous because you are well loved in this family.

"Yes, her husband works closely with the emperor. But he does not have as much of his ear as Selina would like to think, and frankly, he would not be interested in this sorry tale. Do not let it worry you."

The deacon turned to her. "She's well known as a scold and would like to be more important than she really is. Pay no attention to what she said. You're modest and faithful, and God knows your heart. Don't let her ugly words hurt you."

"And besides, Macrina," said Basil, "I have good news! We might be able to get our house and property back! It will take some time, but Peter and Flavius will work on it for us."

"Flavius is back?" She said the words, but barely paid attention to them. She was still reeling from Selina's attack.

"No, not yet, but Peter will send a letter."

"In the meantime, you can both stay with us, here," said Bishop Peter, making yet another offer.

She looked from one to the other, uneasy and too upset to think. All she wanted to do was hide and cry, and pray for forgiveness for whatever truth there was in Selina's words.

"That's kind of you, Peter, but I still think it safer if we make our own arrangements," said Basil. He put an arm protectively around his wife. Macrina nodded gratefully at Basil's response, and the reassuring warmth. "You know that we are marked. Especially now that Selina is upset at Macrina, we don't want to bring any more risk upon you or others than already exists. Anyone caught harboring us would be in trouble."

Peter looked from one to the other, kindness and understanding in his face. "If ever you do change your minds, my friends, knock and the door will be opened. At the very least, be sure to stop by each day for a meal. Macrina, put her words out of your mind. She spoke nothing but lies."

Chapter Fifteen
Advent 311

The weather through most of the year and a half since they'd lost their property had been miserable. If it wasn't rainy, it was grey and cold and damp—the bone-chilling damp that wouldn't go away, with only the occasional run of bright sunny days. Macrina shivered again and sneezed.

Head and eyes downcast, she walked rapidly down the road, doing her best to appear as nothing more than a poor freedwoman, out on an errand for her employer.

It was hard, though. A lifetime of upright, regal pride and bearing, as well as her excitement at seeing Claudia for the first time in several months, ensured she had to constantly remind herself to walk humbly.

The rain sleeted down, soaking Macrina's hair and splashing on the pavement. She hurried, slipping on the wet stone. The rain was icy cold and heavy, and within minutes she was soaked. Her *lacerna*—a workingman's woolen cloak—draped over her shoulders and down to her knees, with a hood she could pull over her head. While it was fine for cold, still weather, the open sides, to allow freedom of movement, did nothing to keep her either warm or dry in this wind.

She paused at the corner, cursing as a passing cart splashed her. In spite of the rain, the street was crowded. As in many parts of the empire, Neocaesareans lived most of their lives in the streets, shopping, eating, drinking, gossiping, and in some cases, like Macrina and Basil, sleeping and cooking in them. She drew her hood over her head and held it under her chin as she glanced right and left. There didn't appear to be anyone particularly interested in her, but she took no chances. In keeping with her tattered, humble appearance, she turned at the alley and walked rapidly down to the servants' entrance of Claudia's house.

The slave knew her and admitted her immediately. He led her straight to the dining room, where she warmed her hands at the brazier.

As she held her hands over the glowing charcoal, Macrina looked around. To reflect his official status, Flavius's house was richly decorated. Bright floor tiles and brilliantly executed wall frescoes enlivened every room.

Her favorite fresco in all the house was right across the room from her.

It appeared, to the untrained eye, to depict the goddess Demeter giving a banquet. In the foreground, she directed the overseer, while several servants carrying large *amphoras* of wine stood by. In the background the guests obviously enjoyed the party.

But the fact that the overseer stood in the open door of the house, with the sun behind him creating a halo, and the fact that the woman directing him appeared, when Macrina looked closely, to be bowing to him, told her that this illustrated the story of the wedding at Cana, when Jesus had first revealed His power. All Claudia's frescoes were as cleverly and subtly done.

She turned as Claudia herself glided into the room.

"Macrina! It's so good to see you." Claudia hurried up, beaming. The women embraced. Macrina stifled a pang of envy for the obvious softness and warmth of Claudia's thick woolen dalmatica.

"You're wet and freezing!" declared Claudia. "Your hands are like ice, and your clothes are soaked through. Into the bath with you, this instant!"

A blissful few hours later, Macrina reclined on a couch in the dining room, sipping heated wine, nibbling some nuts and bread. She was clean and dressed in a warm woolen tunic, while her own dried. Warm from the bones out, she curled up on the dining couch, cozier than anytime since they'd been turned out of their home. Claudia had brought letters from Mus up from Caesarea, and Macrina read them while she ate the bread, reveling in the news and events of his life. She folded them and put them aside as Claudia entered the dining room and sat in the mater's chair.

"You look better, like the old Macrina, before all the troubles. Was the hairdresser adequate? She didn't do a very good job, I must say."

"It's fine, Claudia. I wouldn't let her. It would attract too much attention for a humble freedwoman to have a head of hair like a rich matron."

Claudia slumped back in her chair, her face reflecting her disappointment at Macrina's refusal. Then she leaned forward eagerly.

"I have some dalmaticas and tunics, and some shoes for you," she said. "And I'm having a basket of food made up. The slave will bring them in a few minutes."

Macrina put her goblet on the table and shifted uneasily. "Thank you, Claudia, but I really can't accept them."

"Why not?"

"They're—you're—it's—it wouldn't be suitable—the clothes you wear are far too fine for me. And besides, I'd feel awful—they'd be ruined in no time and I'd hate to do that to such lovely things," Macrina said awkwardly. She appreciated the offer, but it made her profoundly uncomfortable.

"And the food?" Claudia's tone was cool and she sat upright in her chair.

"Oh, yes, the food, please, and thank you."

"No doubt you can give it to some of the other homeless Christians?"

Claudia's tone made her pause. That was exactly what Macrina meant to do. What was wrong with that, she wondered, but Claudia jumped up from her chair and paced around the room. "You are the most stiff-necked, proud, impossible-to-help woman I've ever met," she exclaimed.

Macrina just looked at her.

"Don't you love me?" asked Claudia.

"Of course I do. You're my best and oldest friend!"

"Then let me repay you."

"Repay me? What do you mean, Claudia? You owe me nothing."

"Who stood by my side and argued with my parents when I wanted to marry a totally unsuitable man? Who was there the instant after they'd killed him, and left me a widow after only three months of marriage? Who took me into her home and held me while I cried? Who gave

109

me a reason to live, and then arranged my marriage to Flavius? Who comforted me year after year, when I lost baby after baby?" demanded Claudia.

"But that was just friendship! You'd have done the same for me."

"But I've never had the chance," Claudia said, leaning over and holding out her hands beseechingly. Her eyes were shiny with unshed tears. "All those years, you gave and gave and gave and never once did you ask for anything in return. Never once did you need anything I could give you. Now, when I can help you and make your life easier, you won't accept it." Claudia turned away, facing the brazier at the back of the room. Her shoulders shook.

"But it puts you at such risk."

Claudia laughed harshly and turned back to Macrina, wiping her eyes. "Oh, yes, such incredible risk to give you a warm woolen tunic or two that anyone could have bought. A couple of pairs of shoes, and a basket of food that could have come from anywhere—I'm in such terrible danger. I can hear the soldiers at the door now!"

Macrina sat, stunned. She'd never heard this tone, this anger and pain, from her friend before.

"And there's something else to think of, if you won't count friendship. You're in grave danger of falling into sin, Macrina."

"Sin? What do you mean?" Macrina sat up, indignant. "How am I sinning?"

"Pride. You're too proud to accept what others offer you."

"That's not true, Claudia!" Macrina stood up, bristling. "Don't you understand? How can you think that I'd be too proud to accept care and comfort from you?

110

It simply puts people at too much risk. Should I carry the responsibility for your death if the soldiers arrest you because I've accepted your hospitality and your food and clothing?"

"Then why are you here at all?"

"You sent for me. You said you had letters and you did and I've read them and you're wonderful for bringing them and I am in your debt, because I'd never hear of my boy except from you!"

"Little enough that is! Macrina, if you won't see your pride, then think of this—will you deny me the chance to practice a virtue?"

"What do you mean?"

"Charity. By helping you, I'm denying myself—I'm doing what is good for you, with no regard for my own comfort or safety. That is good in the eyes of the Lord, and you're not letting me do that. You're denying me a chance to come closer to God."

Macrina sat heavily on the couch, blinking, shocked all over again. She'd never thought of it that way before. What right did she have to deny Claudia the chance to become a better Christian? To give back some of the love and concern she'd received from Macrina over the years? To help when Macrina really could use help? And if it was a risk, wasn't that part of God's plan, perhaps? Was she, Macrina, guilty of the sin of pride? Of being too stiff-necked to accept help from other Christians, especially her best friend?

She sat, thinking about all of this, while Claudia sat quietly beside her.

"I love you more than anyone except God and Flavius," Claudia said quietly. She took Macrina's hand in her own and rubbed it gently. "But I can't stand seeing you in such awful circumstances, knowing that I can help, knowing I can do much to ease your misery and hardship, if only you'd let me. I'm sorry to speak so harshly, but I couldn't stay quiet any more."

Macrina nodded, her throat too constricted to speak.

"Is it really so hard to accept a tunic and shoes and

some food—for you, not for everyone else? Would it be so hard to accept our—or Bishop Peter's, or Simeon's, or Olivia's—offer to stay with us, out of the cold and the wet?

"Come live with us," she pleaded, eyes alight with the pleasure of the idea. "You would be safe, you'd be warm and clothed and fed, and you'd have nothing to worry about. Do it, please. We'd be so happy to have you."

Macrina looked at her friend, Claudia's figure blurry because of the tears rolling down her cheeks. She swallowed and took a deep breath. "I will accept the clothes and the food, Claudia, with thanks. Grateful thanks. But I can't put you at such risk by living with you. It's only through God's grace Flavius has been able to keep his faith and his post. I don't want to put you in that kind of danger."

Claudia leaned forward again as another idea struck her. "But the new edict! It was proclaimed last May—the Edict of Toleration. Surely they wouldn't dare do anything now. Both Augustus Constantine and Augustus Licinius have said we are to be let alone to worship, as long as we include prayers for the health of them and the empire!"

"Claudia. You know as well as I do that it's only toleration. Christianity is not legal, and the enforcement of the edict depends on the governors."

"Meaning," Claudia sighed and leaned back, "that it won't change much here. But who would know? We could—"

"We are known, Claudia. We are marked. The tribune said as much when he threw us out. People note where we go and to whom we speak, and they make sure that those in power find out. It was a risk, coming here today, but I missed you so much that I couldn't resist.

"If we were to live with you, how long do you think Flavius would stay in the governor's confidence, or even free? And don't forget—Selina is still trying to have me declared a traitor to the faith! If she thought you were aiding me, you and Flavius would be in even more danger."

"You don't think she'd denounce us, surely?"

"I do think so. Look at what misery she's causing poor Godarius."

The soldier had met with Simeon as Macrina had arranged, and taken instruction from him ever since. He would be admitted to the catechumenate after Pascha. But Selina, in her jealousy and because of her humiliation in front of the bishop, was determined to make Macrina's life miserable. She lied and gossiped about it to everyone who knew Macrina and had a special resentment for Godarius, the poor man. At least half the congregation were so suspicious of him they would have nothing to do with him.

"It's a testament to his courage that he can stand the trouble she's caused," said Claudia.

"It is indeed, but if she's doing that to him, do you think she'd just wink at you taking us in? She likes you, and so it would be doubly hard for her to bear, to think that she'd failed in supplanting me in your affections."

"I know," Claudia said, slumping back in her chair again. "But honestly, Macrina, I'd risk it for you. It breaks my heart to see you reduced to nothing more than a—a beggar! I long to do something for you."

Claudia's voice broke and she pursed her lips and turned her head away.

Macrina sat up and embraced her friend. "Oh, my dear," she said, her own voice thick with emotion, "thank

God for you! You are such a blessing and such a gift."

"Me?" Claudia half laughed and half sobbed. "Why me? I sit here, warm, rich, and comfortable, while you freeze and are tormented. I'd think you'd despise me for being such a coward."

"You," Macrina said firmly. "You and Flavius would risk all you have, your home, his position, even your lives, to give us a home and a warm place to sleep. Knowing you love me enough to risk your life for my bodily comfort—I can't tell you how much that means to me, how cherished it makes me feel."

"I'm glad, Macrina. I just want to help, especially since Selina blocked Flavius so thoroughly from getting your property back."

Flavius had delivered the bad news a month ago, and Basil had been devastated.

Macrina sighed. "If there is any way that woman can cause us grief, she will. We appreciate him trying, though."

"Aren't you disappointed?"

"Basil is. He had his heart set on this idea the very day we lost everything. And I'm disappointed for his sake. But me, no, not really. I think I knew it was gone—any hope was a faint one, and with Selina so adamant about me, and with her husband so high-ranking, I knew it would never happen, so I never gave it any thought. Did Flavius come back from Caesarea with you? I know he's been back and forth without you a lot."

Claudia nodded. "We came up together this time, but will have to go back again very soon. His sister is worse, and we don't expect her to live. But out of it, sad though it is, we might have a child!"

Macrina sat up, startled. "You're—"

Claudia laughed. "No, no! I'm sorry—it's his niece. His sister is a widow, and if she dies, as we expect, we will raise her daughter, Emmelia. She's just three years old. It will be so good to have a daughter."

"That would be wonderful!" Macrina said, delighted for her friend. "After all these years, you'll have a child."

"Mistress?"

Claudia turned to the slave waiting in the doorway, a large covered basket in her arms, Macrina's dry lacerna and tunic draped over the top. "Yes, put it over there."

The servant bowed and raised the basket. "Yes, mistress. Also, a tribune is at the door."

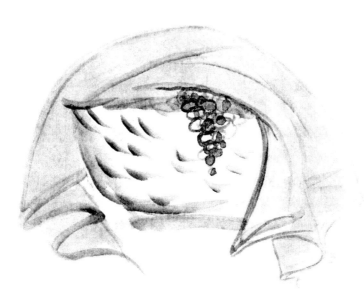

Chapter Seventeen
Advent 311

Claudia darted to her feet, her face paling.
"Quickly, Macrina, into the corner." She took
the basket and shoved it into Macrina's arms,
dragged her to her feet, and pushed her into the corner
furthest from the doorway.

"Stay there until he leaves."

Claudia strode out of the room. Macrina crept to the
doorway and glanced between the dining room and the
hall to the servant's door. The house was laid out around
the central atrium, and every door and hall led off it.

There was no way she could leave the dining room without being seen from the entry hall, but she had to try. If she were found here, it could be disastrous for her friends.

She drew back into the corner and slipped the lacerna on. The basket of food she clutched close to her chest, under the cloak, and listened intently.

"Flavius, I want wine and I want it warm. Claudia, this is governor's business." The blustery voice filled the spacious atrium and rolled into the rooms grouped around it. The tribune's presence crowded the large space, and his voice invaded corners and pressed against the walls.

Macrina crept to the door and her heart sank as she got a glimpse of the man—she'd never forget that face—it was the same one who'd overseen their eviction.

"Here, here, just here," Flavius said, following the large, red-faced officer. He glanced into the dining room, pointed to himself and the tribune, then to the study, and finally, gestured to Macrina and toward the side exit, down the hall that lay across the atrium from her. Macrina nodded and waited anxiously until they'd disappeared.

She sped across the atrium toward the servant's door.

"Here, you! Wait!" shouted the officer.

Macrina stopped, shivering in fear.

"Flavius, don't you know this is a Christian?" he asked in horror, striding from the study. Flavius hurried after him and tore the basket of food and clothing from Macrina's hands. He tossed it at a slave. "Take this," the secret Christian ordered. He turned back to the army officer and shook his head, pretending an equal horror. "I never even knew she was here. Had the slave told me, I'd never have let her in or given her food. I'll send her away at once!"

The tribune put out his hand. "Just a moment. You know," he said, turning to Macrina, "if you were to offer that pinch of incense, you could have all your belongings and property back. All it takes is one small pinch. Renounce your god and be a Roman again."

Macrina drew herself up and gathered her poor clothing about her. "I *am* a Roman, Tribune. I'm a Christian Roman. I owe allegiance to the Triune God before Rome, before anything. All we live for is to glorify and praise Him. He has been good to us—we have food and we find shelter. He looks after us, my Basil and me."

"Oh, yes, just look at you," the army officer sneered. He shook his head and gestured at her old, hand-me-down clothing. "Look at those fancy new shoes, and your fine silken tunic! You're doing very well."

Macrina blushed and smoothed her hand down the simple woolen robe. Her feet were bare.

"You were important in this town once, and I know you were held in high esteem among the other Christians. Now look—you're destitute. How can you think you're better off? Those Christian friends of yours aren't helping. Look at you!"

He walked around her, sneering and gloating over her downfall. In truth, she did look shabby against the fine wool of Flavius's clothing and the smart imperial uniform the tribune wore. The tunic she was wearing was old, and while clean, was patched near the hem. Claudia had packed the nice ones, and her own pride had demanded the lesser one after her bath. The worn and threadbare lacerna seemed even more faded and shabby against the bright mosaics and painted scenes around her, even in the gloom of a rainy afternoon. Still, she stood proudly, not letting the commander see how his words hurt.

"We are fed, and we are clothed. We praise God, and we have each other. That is all we need." She glanced through her lashes at Flavius, who was still scowling at her in pretended anger, then looked down at the floor again. "And our brothers do not forsake us in our time of need, Commander.

"My Basil is still a Reader. Our poverty makes no difference in the community. And, if we die in poverty, we still have God, and His love is worth more than the emperor's palace and all it contains."

The officer spat at her feet and turned away.

"I don't know why you aren't all executed. If it were up to me, I would, even with the new edict. Get out of my sight—and you, Flavius, you better take more care, or people will start asking questions about you!"

Flavius glanced at the commander, but he had already returned to the study. Then he grabbed Macrina's arm and hustled her along the hall to the side door.

"I'm sorry, Flavius," she said, in a whisper.

"It couldn't be helped," he replied. "You aren't to worry—did you get enough to eat? I'll have her bring the basket out to you—wait by the door."

"No it's too much—" She stopped, remembering Claudia's words. "Yes, thank you, you're kind, but be careful. You've taken enough of a risk already. Should he even have a shadow of suspicion, you'd lose everything."

Flavius bowed to her. "Wait here, she'll be out in a moment. I just wish we could do more. Anything we have is yours."

Impulsively, she hugged him. Flavius blushed and nodded, then said in a loud, angry voice, "Now get out and don't come back, you piece of filth." He dropped to a whisper again. "God go with you."

"And you, Flavius." She shut the side door and moved into the cold rain on the street to wait for the basket.

Chapter Eighteen
Late Summer 313

There he is!" Basil pointed across the street and waved to Godarius. He'd been waiting in the street for them ever since the "Catechumens depart" instruction in the liturgy. Normally, Macrina and Basil looked forward to the feast after liturgy, but today, Godarius promised he'd treat them to a meal. An inn he frequented specialized in his native Hispania dishes, and he wanted to introduce them to his favorites.

After the meal, they wandered through the city, with most of the rest of the population. It was late summer, the days were long, and they had all afternoon to spend as they wished.

They were approaching the forum when a commotion down the street distracted them. A babbling crowd loomed close, followed by a squad of soldiers. From their appearance, and from the lines of clerks and functionaries following them, with the governor bringing up the rear of the procession, it looked as though there was some kind of official announcement to be read from the steps of the government building.

"What's going on?" asked Macrina.

Godarius shook his head. "I was given the day off today, as usual. There was something about a pronouncement and a parade through to the forum, but no one knew why."

"Flavius said nothing, and usually he knows, if anyone does," commented Basil.

"Shall we follow and find out what's going on?" Godarius asked.

There was no need even to ask the question, really—pronouncements were not frequent events, and all three of them were curious.

Basil grabbed Macrina's hand and hauled her into the square with the rest of the populace. The governor's escort marched through the crowd, pushing aside those who weren't quick enough to get out of the way. She saw slaves and citizens alike scurrying out to the side or being bowled over by the soldiers of the governor's guard.

She, Basil, and Godarius edged toward the government building.

"I heard there's a new emperor, Constantine's been assassinated!" said one bald, elderly gentleman.

"Nonsense! Constantine and Licinius have finally fought it out, and Licinius has been victorious. So my uncle told me, and he's in the government and is high in the governor's regard." This from a young man next to the bald fellow.

He must be related to Selina, thought Macrina.

"Constantine was killed in the battle," commented a woman in a red dalmatica.

"Don't be stupid! I heard that he defeated Licinius, and he's now sole emperor."

The knot of political speculators argued as Macrina pushed past them.

"That dead Jew's faith is finally being outlawed, once and for all. All the Christians are to be rounded up and killed," sniffed an elaborately coiffed woman whose palla was silk.

Macrina went cold at the thought. Hadn't there been enough persecution? Nearly three hundred years! In spite of the Edict of Toleration two years ago, her life hadn't changed much. Licinius was no friend of the Christians, and neither was the governor of Pontus. They more or less ignored the Edict. She wiggled past the woman, who sniffed and drew back from Macrina's humble appearance as if from a pile of garbage. Macrina scarcely noticed as she hurried to keep up with the men.

"Christianity's being legalized," said one hopeful, making the sign of the cross. In full, public view, too, Macrina noticed, scandalized.

There were more and even wilder speculations, from an increase in taxes—*and since when had that ever needed a proclamation,* thought Macrina—to invaders on the doorstep.

They pushed their way to the front of the crowd, as close to the steps as they could get.

Basil pulled her away from the soldiers as they mounted the steps. They were followed by the dignitaries—Flavius among them. He was pale and looked shaken. Macrina chewed her lip as she began to worry. Maybe the woman had it right—perhaps Constantine wasn't such a friend after all, and had lured them with the tolerance, only to revert to the terror once again.

The trumpet fanfare silenced the crowd. The governor, flanked by Selina's husband on one side and Flavius on the other, and backed by all the full-toga'd and official-looking men the city could find, stepped forward and unrolled a large, be-ribboned, elaborate scroll.

It was as if, Macrina thought, whoever had written it for the emperor wanted it to look as important as the words inside.

The trumpets blared again, and the drums rumbled their deep tones, so loud Macrina could feel them underfoot.

In the silence, the governor began to speak, expertly projecting his deep, slow voice to all corners of the forum.

Macrina scarcely listened to the preamble, catching only bits and pieces. "Constantine Augustus, as well as I Licinius Augustus . . . met near Mediolanum."

Hurry up, she thought, *get to the important part!*

She gave a start when she heard, "those regulations pertaining to the reverence of the Divinity." Her heart began thumping in her chest as the governor continued, "so that we might grant to the Christians and others full authority to observe that religion which each preferred . . ." The world spun around her, and she grabbed Basil's arm. Distractedly, he put his arm around her and held her close against his side.

It couldn't be true, could it? The governor continued, "We thought to arrange that no one whatsoever should be denied the opportunity to give his heart to the observance of the Christian religion," and "any one of these who wishes to observe the Christian religion might do so freely and openly, without molestation."

She swayed against Basil. They were free; finally and totally and completely free. Macrina stood in stunned silence, too overwhelmed by the knowledge and sudden release to completely absorb the news.

"'Oh come hither and behold the works of the Lord, what wonders has He wrought upon the earth,'" she murmured. "'He makes wars to cease in all the world; He breaks the bow and snaps the shield of armor in sunder and burns the shields in the fire.'" Tears streamed down her face as she quoted from the Psalms.

"Listen, there's more," Basil hushed her.

"Moreover, in the case of the Christians especially we esteemed it best to order . . . those places where they were previously accustomed to assemble, . . . the same shall be restored to the Christians without payment or any claim of recompense and without any kind of fraud or deception."

"'Be still then, and know that I am God; I will be

129

exalted among the nations and I will be exalted in the earth. The Lord of Hosts is with us, the God of Jacob is our refuge.'" Macrina's voice rose, ending in a shout which was picked up and echoed by the Christians in the crowd. "'The Lord of hosts is with us; the God of Jacob is our refuge!' Blessed be the name of the Lord, henceforth and forevermore! Blessed be the name of the Lord, henceforth and forevermore!"

The shouts of the Christians drowned out the governor's voice, and he had to wait until the crowd quieted. Macrina didn't listen to the rest of the proclamation; she was too filled with joy and wonder, crying uncontrollably at the still-shocking reality, until Basil picked her up by the elbows and whirled her in the air.

"Did you hear? Did you hear? Not only are we legal, we get all our property back! Macrina, truly the Lord is good!"

"Blessed be the Lord, henceforth and forevermore!"

Section Three
At Peace

•

Chapter Nineteen
Late Spring 325

At dawn, Macrina stood on the stairs to the main floor of Claudia's home in Caesarea. She squeezed Emmelia's hand and kissed her cheek. Emmelia, her features blurred by the flame-colored veil, gave her a shaky smile. Below, they could hear the priest asking for God's blessing on the day.

Mus waited in the atrium, with the priest and the assembled guests, for Macrina to bring his bride to him.

The priest pronounced the "Amen" and Macrina led Emmelia down the last few stairs and through the crowd to Mus's side.

She reached for her son's hand, her own trembling, her eyesight blurred with tears. Though the hand she grasped was large, strong, and capable, a man's hand, it still somehow retained a memory of the child's hand—small, fine-boned, and delicate. She placed Emmelia's hand in Mus's and stepped back to her own husband's side, nodding at the young girl.

Emmelia looked panic-stricken for a moment and glanced over at her aunt. Claudia, smiling broadly, her eyes sparkling with unshed tears, nodded also. The bride turned back to her betrothed.

"Wh-When and where you are, Gaius, th-then and there I am, Gaia." Emmelia spoke the traditional words of consent in a quavery, high voice. Macrina was proud of her. Sixteen years old and able to handle herself this well on the most momentous day of her life. She had accepted the marriage with a good heart, even though she wanted to remain a virgin, dedicated to the Lord. Claudia had raised her niece well. Emmelia was devout and possessed good solid common sense. Flavius's sister could rest in peace, assured that her brother and his wife had been good parents.

Macrina felt *her* Basil's hand enfold her own as the priest offered the blessings of the church and prayers for a happy and fruitful marriage. She glanced up at the older man next to her and remembered thinking in their exile how her little Mus had resembled his father. Now, looking at the two of them, she blinked. It could be her husband standing at the bride's side, as she remembered him from their own marriage day.

The older man, in his turn, had aged with dignity and grace—his grey hair topped a figure tall and straight. The lines on his face and neck, the veins in his hands and the wiry muscles gave him an added air of wisdom and competence.

He was looking tired, she realized. Handsome, dignified, but grey in the face and neck. He bent down, squeezed her hand gently, and whispered, "When and where you are, Gaia, then and there—" He broke off, coughing harshly. The cough was under control in a few seconds, but to Macrina's ear, it sounded wet and deep, and his face, she noted with a tinge of alarm, had gone a deep red.

She looked at him with worry, but he took her hand and patted it. "Then and there I am, Gaius," he finished.

She chided herself for the heat she felt rising in her face. She, mother of a wedded man, to blush like her new daughter-in-law!

Still, she thought to herself, she was growing old well. Silver threads wove through her dark hair, and when she looked in the bronze mirror she saw creases on her neck and around her eyes and mouth, but not, she felt, so many as other women her age. The backs of her hands showed a few pale brown spots, and the chilly mornings here in Neocaesarea meant that it took longer to get out of bed, until the stiffness subsided. But overall, she felt as energetic and lively as ever. She smiled up at her Basil as she listened to the prayers.

God was good—He'd given her hardships, certainly, but they'd been balanced by good health, a loving family, and twelve years of peace since the Edict of Milan had been proclaimed.

She shook herself mentally as the guests surged forward to congratulate the couple, then worked her way slowly to the center of the crowd. It was large, packing the roomy atrium, spilling into the dining room and out into the courtyard garden. It felt to Macrina as though all of the city were here. Mus was a popular lawyer and public speaker and had made many friends. There was family, too, their own relatives—Basil's brother and his grown children and grandchildren, as well as Claudia's and Flavius's brothers and sisters, and Emmelia's brothers and their families.

"Thank you," the bride said, when Macrina finally reached the couple. Emmelia threw her arms around Macrina's neck and squeezed tightly. "Thank you for Basil, and for being *pronuba*. You were so calm on the stairs. I was so nervous, I thought I'd forget the words."

Macrina hugged her back just as warmly. "I'm delighted to have you as my daughter. You'll make an ideal wife for Mus, and you did wonderfully. Enjoy your day, my dear, and revel in your friends. They are God's gift to you."

"No less than you, Mater," she replied. "I thank Him daily, for Basil and for such wonderful parents as Aunt Claudia and Uncle Flavius. I was so grateful they

136

accepted Basil when you spoke to them about it." She seemed about to say more, but her attention was taken by someone next to Macrina.

Macrina turned to Mus, her throat thickening and her eyes misting again. Her heart was so full she couldn't speak, so she touched his cheek instead. He took her hand and kissed it gently, then put his arms around her.

"If Emmelia and I have half as good a marriage as you and Papa, I'll feel like the most blessed man in the empire," he whispered in her ear. "Pray for us."

"Every day, my love, I promise," she said. "For children, and joy and blessings. For only enough sorrow to highlight your happiness."

"Thank you, Mama. For everything."

She smiled through her tears and shook her head. "No. Thank God. I just tried to do what He showed me."

M acrina indulged herself with oysters on their shell, set on lettuce so green and crisp it seemed to be still growing.

"Have some of the **garum sauce**," said Claudia, as she sat down next to Macrina. "It's wonderful." Around them, people walked and talked, sat on the raised concrete edge of the garden, drinking wine and eating, or simply enjoying the music and the wonderful summer weather.

"I know, I already did—and Godarius gets all our business."

"How is he?"

"Fine. His import business is thriving since he left the army, and his children are thriving even more."

"When did he leave the army, Macrina? I don't remember. Eight years or so, hasn't it been?"

"No, more like eleven. Let's see. Emmelia came to you just after Constantine issued the edict, and Godarius left the army just after that. He started the import business then and was baptized—two years after that, I think."

"Where does he get such good-quality food?"

"His family makes it, and he ships it here. He has contacts who produce all kinds of special food that's made only where he grew up."

Claudia looked around, then leaned toward Macrina. "I heard about Selina the other day."

Macrina raised an eyebrow as she tore a strip of tender white meat from a chicken breast. She popped it in her mouth and nodded at Claudia.

"She's still trying to make everyone believe how important she is. She and her husband are in Byzantium—he's apparently in charge of the construction of the new city—Constantinople."

Macrina tried not to laugh with a mouthful of chicken. She'd heard the news, of course, how the little, relatively backward town was to become the "New Rome" once Constantine's building plans were realized.

"I heard it's nothing but mud and pigs," she said after she'd swallowed.

Claudia nodded, her eyes glinting merrily. "I doubt that Selina will be happy there."

"At least she's not here," Macrina said. "Speaking of pigs, come into the dining room with me. I thought I saw some loin of pork, and I haven't had that for a long time."

They moved into the dining room, where the bridal couple reclined on the couch of honor. Across from them, Basil had saved a spot for Macrina. She helped herself to more food and lay next to her husband, joining in the general conversation and laughter.

Toward the end of the afternoon, she noticed Mus and some of his friends slip away. She smiled to herself, as the flute and lyre began the wedding hymn. It was taken up by the guests. The timing was ragged, the individual voices as variable as the meal's dishes had been, and her own thin, high warble added nothing to the quality of the music. But to Macrina's ear, the collection of voices filling the room sounded like a choir of angels.

A few moments after the last notes of the song died away, wild cries broke out from the garden, and screams from the servants echoed through the atrium and into the dining room. Before they'd had time to fade, a party of men rushed in. The remaining guests screamed and shouted, fending off in good-natured rough-housing the attack of the groom and his men.

Claudia, screaming in mock terror, scrambled from her couch and threw her arms around Emmelia.

"No, no, you shall not have my daughter," she proclaimed, playing the outraged and courageous mother.

"Hah! I shall have her," Basil countered from the doorway, enjoying the game as much as his new mother-in-law. "She will be mine, do you hear? Mine!" He leaped onto the nearest couch as guests scrambled out of the way, throwing flowers and food at him and his band of men—who were laughing too hard to assist him.

He advanced toward his bride, stepping on couches,

141

tripping on his formally wrapped toga, and spilling a decanter of wine over his employer, who promptly grabbed it and took a swig. Mus climbed over prone bodies, careless of the wine goblets he kicked or the food he trampled on.

As he stepped off the last couch, Claudia thrust the laughing Emmelia behind her and raised a hand to ward off the intruder.

"You shall not have her," she proclaimed, every inch the outraged, brave Roman matron, fending off the barbarian intruder.

"Away, woman, your daughter is mine!" Basil growled.

Claudia swung round and gathered Emmelia in her arms. "Never, do you hear? Never will I give her up!"

Basil grabbed his new wife's arm and tugged gently, while managing to convey an impressive performance of rough and hostile intent. The effect was somewhat ruined by Emmelia's giggles, and the ease with which Claudia surrendered her "daughter."

The newly married pair bounded back over the couches and guests and escaped into the atrium. The entire wedding party tumbled after them. There, with the priest and her new husband, waited Emmelia, now attended by three young boys.

Led by the priest and the bridal pair, accompanied by the musicians, the party moved into the street and set off for Basil and Emmelia's new home.

The procession swelled on the journey, as passersby and neighbors joined the crowd and added to the merriment. The groom distributed the nuts tradition demanded, to ensure a fruitful union, before he darted down a side-street, unnoticed by most of the guests. It was the custom that he should arrive at their new home first, to greet his bride and guests.

Macrina noted with approval that Basil was standing by the open doorway as the now huge procession reached the house. She was pleased with how calmly and competently Emmelia wound the doorposts with the bright red wool she herself had spun, anointed the door with oil and fat, and repeated her words of consent to fulfill the traditions. Macrina smiled and blinked back tears of both joy and a melancholy nostalgia as her son, her no-longer-little Mus, carefully lifted his bride and carried her over the threshold of their home.

BASIL AND EMMELIA SET THE TONE of their life right away. They were generous with their hospitality, often opening their house for gatherings of their friends and family because it was a warm sunny day, or because it was a cold, snowy one and people needed to be cheered up. Macrina and Basil spent much time at the house, often with Claudia and Flavius there as well. They would enjoy a good meal and spend the afternoon and evening in long talks about the faith and politics, discussing, among other things, the upcoming council to be held in August, in Nicea. It was the first of its kind since the Apostles' council in Jerusalem, several hundred years before, and every bishop in Christendom, it seemed, was going to be present.

"Three hundred, I heard last," said Basil one evening over dinner.

"However many do attend, it will be good to get the faith solidified," replied Macrina. "This Arius is causing far too much dissent. Even Bishop Gaius is beginning to give credence to his views!" Bishop Peter had died the previous spring, and Gaius was his replacement.

Flavius snorted. "Too many of them are Arians already, and they say Augustus Constantine himself is inclined toward them." He shook his head and snorted again. "The Son is created and isn't co-equal to the Father. What nonsense!"

"Well, I'm sure they'll correct him at the council," remarked Claudia. "After all, he hasn't that much support, has he?"

"I hope not," replied Macrina thoughtfully, "but many of our people seem to think his theories more understandable than the truth."

Basil shook his head. "It's not that simple, though. It's not just the two positions. There are a number of bishops who stand between the two extremes, and it's getting them to see that they're closer to Athanasius's position of God and Christ being identical in essence, rather than Arius's. Some of the bishops object to the term Athanasius uses, because it's been used in the past by heretics, and they're afraid of it. It's not going to be an easy decision, one way or the other."

"Even if they do find agreement, there's still Meletius and his supporters," said Flavius.

Macrina nodded. "That's not an easy one either. It's all very well to say 'forgive,' but it's harder to do when you see people who burned the incense and recanted wanting to be accepted back as if nothing had happened."

"But Christ did tell us to forgive seventy times seven," said Emmelia, raising herself on her elbows. "I know it's hard. We've all lost people, and you've suffered because you wouldn't concede, but we're all in need of forgiveness. We aren't perfect, none of us. If the church assumes we must be, the church is going to be a display of saints, not a hospital for the broken and hurt. Christ came to save sinners, not the righteous. There won't be room for any of us if Meletius has his way."

Mus picked up his goblet. "I'm just glad, right now, that we don't have to decide for the church. They're difficult issues, but tonight isn't the night to debate them. Did you hear what Flavius said about the buildings in Constantinople?"

Chapter Twenty-One
Late Pentecost 325

It was late summer, and Basil and Macrina sat on the terrace of the country villa in the warm morning sun. Birds sang in the trees, and the air was scented with late summer flowers.

"And what does today hold?" asked Macrina.

"The overseer and I need to talk about the grape harvest," said Basil. "It's almost time, and we need to keep an eye on them, he said. And he wants to talk about the farm in general, so we'll probably be out most of the day, seeing to the shepherds and the crops." He winced and massaged his chest.

"Sounds like a busy day then," Macrina said. "Would I be in the way if I came along?"

"It would be a pleasure," he said, getting to his feet. He walked toward the stairs at the end of the terrace. Raised beds surrounded the patio, the earth held back by calf-high marble walls topped by a marble railing, just wide and high enough to sit on. At the far end, where Basil stood now, grew a small herb garden. Not intended for the kitchen, it was a bed of the aromatic herbs they found most enjoyable. He stopped at the bed and plucked a piece of his namesake.

"Am I as peppery—" He took a deep breath, and sat suddenly and heavily on the railing by the raised, formal bed.

"Basil, what is it?" Macrina moved to him as quickly as she could.

"Ah—it hurts, here," he gasped, gripping the left side of his chest.

"Mus!" Macrina called, as loudly as she could, then to her husband, "No, my love, just sit. We'll get the physician. Just wait."

Oh, God, please, she thought, *give me strength to submit to Your will, but please, not yet.*

The servants moved Basil back to their bedroom. The physician came, tut-tutted, and left again, looking gloomy. He talked about Basil's heart and his age, but Macrina didn't need to be told. All she wanted to do was sit beside him, hold his hand, and pray. Once again, she lost track of time. She ate when food appeared and slept when her eyes would no longer stay open. She took no notice of whether it was daylight or lamplight that illuminated his drawn, gray features.

He lay in bed, in pain and only awake for moments in the day following the attack. Then he smiled at her, and they said the prayers together, singing the evening hymn even though it was morning. His low, melodic voice quavered like an old man's, and he gasped for breath on every other word, but it still steadied her reedy, untuneful voice.

"For meet it is at all times to worship Thee with voices of praise, O Son of God and Giver of life. . . ."

"Macrina, my love, will you send for Bishop Gaius, please?"

Her heart stopped for a second. Deep inside, she screamed. It was a long, plaintive wail that went on and on as she nodded gravely to her husband and quietly left the room.

The silent scream continued as she gave the servant his instructions, as she told her son and his wife.

She was calm on the outside. Grave, as befitted a woman about to say the final goodbye to her life's companion, but composed. Not tearing her hair, or wailing uncontrollably. That would come later. For now, there was the serene, controlled Macrina, sitting by her husband's side. She took his hand and kissed his cheek.

"The bishop will be here," she promised. "It will take time, though. Please don't go till he gets here."

Basil opened his eyes and nodded. His hand squeezed hers.

She sat by his bed, refusing to leave his side for the day it took Bishop Gaius to travel from the city. She spoke to no one but her husband and maintained her calm, marble-like demeanor. Inside, the wailing continued. *Not yet, oh please, Lord! I'm not ready to let go of him.*

Gaius arrived and shooed her out for Basil's last confession. Then, at Basil's bedside, he celebrated the liturgy

for them all. She gripped her love's hand through the whole thing and held him up as he accepted the Body and Blood for the last time.

They all communed, and when the final blessing was given, Basil kissed her, sighed, and was gone.

She held his hand still, but inside, the screaming stopped. Everything in her stopped. Her breath continued to move in and out of her body, and her heart continued to beat, but everything else just—stopped.

Gently, one of them, she was never sure who, removed her hand from his. Someone else slid their arm around her and guided her to a chair on the other side of the room, while bodies came and went, washed and dressed him and moved him downstairs to the atrium.

More bodies came in and changed the bed, making it up tidily. Then there was no one in the room with her. Macrina moved over to the bed. She slipped to her knees, and laid her head on the covers. She could still smell his spicy, masculine odor in the soft woolen blanket. She blinked away tears.

She stroked the white wool. Now, the bed would be cold and feel empty, the morning and evening prayers would sound thin and flat without his voice blending with hers. How could she live without him?

Tears trickled into the blanket under her cheek. Yes, she would see him again—but when? How long would she have to go through her days with this aching hole in her heart, feeling as though she were missing a limb?

She sobbed aloud, her hand crumpling the blanket, her chest aching.

Macrina felt Mus lifting her away from the bed, his arms closing around her.

"Shhh, oh Mother, shhh," he whispered, his voice choking with sorrow.

"I miss him!" she wailed. "I want him back, oh God, please, I want my Basil!"

Macrina's son gathered his mother in his arms and rocked her, crying with her.

She clung to him, her son's arms so different from her husband's, but so similar. The hard muscle, the warmth, the proportions were the same, but they had a young man's strength and energy coursing through them.

He helped Macrina to her feet, wiping her eyes and stroking her hair.

She sat on the edge of the bed and looked up at him. "How am I going to live?" she asked. "Why did God take him? Why not me?"

He knelt beside her and took her hands in his warm, fine-boned ones.

"There are no answers, Mother," he said softly. "Not here, not now. He went when God wanted him, for reasons we don't understand. You taught me that. God does what He wants and doesn't always tell us why. We simply have to love Him and trust Him."

"It's so hard," she whispered.

He laughed heartily, throwing his head back and slapping his thighs. She looked at him, shocked beyond words.

"When has life ever been easy? And when has that ever bothered you? Of course it's hard! It's all hard! But God will be there, and He will send you comfort. You know that."

She nodded, and sighed. "You're right, Mus." She stood up, smoothed the blanket, and sniffed. "But it's going to be the hardest thing I've ever done to live without him."

"I have no doubt of that. But we will be close by. And God will never desert you."

Emmelia, who had been standing on the threshold of the room, entered and gave Macrina a hug. "And someday," her daughter-in-law said, patting her stomach, "there will be grandchildren to occupy your time, and your heart."

Chapter Twenty-Two
325–Advent 331

After the funeral, when Emmelia and Basil returned to Neocaesarea, Macrina drifted in a fog of grief. She dreaded returning to their home in the city, where they'd spent so much time. It was too full of memories of Basil, although being at the villa wasn't much better. It saddened her to remember him sitting in his study, or smelling flowers in the garden, standing by the bed with her first thing in the morning and last thing at night. Her reedy voice, which could no longer hold a tune for five notes running, sounded even thinner and frailer, and wandered even more without his rich deep tones keeping her to the melody.

Neither place satisfied her—everywhere she went,

whether it was the study in the city house or the dining room at the villa, she saw him, smelled him, thought she heard his laugh or his step outside the door. She would catch a glimpse of him turning the corner into the gardens. But it would turn out to be Valerius, the overseer, who looked nothing like her late husband, or merely her eyes and ears playing tricks on her.

She shuttled between the city and the country, staying in one place until she could bear it no longer, then traveling to the other, lethargic and uninterested in anything around her. Finally, more than a year after his death, as the nights shortened and grew cold with the coming of winter, Mus and Emmelia insisted on her presence at their home for dinner one day.

Once they were settled on the couches in the dining room, Basil wasted no time.

"We want you to come live with us. You're miserable in your home and too much alone at Annesi, and we need you here."

Macrina toyed with her spoon and pushed the trout around her plate. She covered it with her lettuce and picked a radish up and crunched it between her teeth. She didn't care, one way or another. "Yes, all right," she said finally.

Basil and Emmelia exchanged glances. "Good," said Emmelia. "It's not just for you though, Mother. I need you here, since Aunt Claudia is so occupied with Uncle Flavius." Flavius had been ill for months, but as dear as he was to her, Macrina had been unable to care much. She knew it was serious and that Claudia was worried, but it couldn't penetrate the fog surrounding her.

"All right." Macrina stirred and looked at her daughter. "What for? You're doing well without me, wouldn't I just be in the way?"

"No, I think you'll be a great help to me. And to the baby when it's born."

A flicker of something stirred in Macrina's heart, and for the first time since Basil had died, she felt the black cloud lift—only for a moment, but her smile was warm and real as she looked at them both. "That will be nice."

"THERE," EMMELIA SAID, smiling up from the bed, as the servant handed Macrina the newborn baby. "Your granddaughter. Thanks be to God, she's healthy."

"And as bald as the old bishop," joked Macrina as

she gazed down at the wrinkled, wailing scrap, tiny arms flailing and face bright red. She beamed at her daughter-in-law.

"Praise God the delivery was as easy as it was," Macrina said.

"Easiest one I've ever seen," commented the midwife as she packed away her things. "And I've been birthing babies since before Maximian was emperor." Behind her, the servants moved the birthing chair out of the room.

"We agreed, Basil and I, that at her baptism, he would give her the name Thekla Macrina."

"St. Paul's friend Thekla?" asked Macrina.

Emmelia nodded. "And Macrina, after you."

"I'm honored," Macrina said, feeling her cheeks go red. She reluctantly handed the crying child to her mother and sat on the edge of the bed. The room, lit by lamps and warmed by a bronze brazier in the corner, felt warm and cozy. "You realize you're not going to be rid of me from now on. I intend to spend a great deal of time with you and my grandchild."

Emmelia shifted and put the baby to her breast. "Good. I wouldn't mind if you stayed with us permanently."

THEKLA MACRINA THRIVED and Macrina enjoyed spending time with her granddaughter. She held her for hours, content to sit and read while the baby slept in the crook of her arm.

She knew she should return to her own home, but every time she mentioned it, both Basil and Emmelia urged her to stay. In due time, Emmelia had another child, a boy this time, whom they called Naucratius. Both Macrina and her namesake welcomed the boy and spent their time looking after him, or concocting toys and games to capture his attention and delight him, and eventually it was an accepted fact that Macrina would stay with her son and his family permanently.

She was besotted with her third grandchild from the moment he was born, and was even more delighted when her son named him Basil, after her husband. She adored the little one—from the way his hair refused to grow on the crown of his head, to his tiny, perfectly formed feet. And he, in his turn, seemed equally charmed by his silver-haired grandmother.

"THE FOUR OF YOU ARE A TERROR," commented Emmelia one warm spring day. She sat down in the sunny garden, where the three children played with Macrina. They chased her around the carefully laid-out walks, searching for her when she hid behind the tall bushes in their pots, then tackling her and tickling each other into helpless giggles.

Thekla Macrina, or the younger Macrina, as the family called her more and more often, was four now. She was conscious of her status as the eldest and tried to act in a dignified and solemn manner. But at the promise of a romp with *Nona*, the dignity was shed, the solemn expression banished for brilliant smiles and a laugh that, to her indulgent grandmother's ears, sounded like the music of the heavenly choir.

Naucratius, all legs and protruding tummy at almost three, had no concept of dignity or solemnity. He spent most of his time trying to induce Nona to put down her book, or her spinning, or leave her visits with Claudia to come and play with him. Usually, both the older women ended up on the floor with the babies.

But it was Basil the baby, just past his first year and walking, who melted Macrina into a small puddle of sentiment whenever he smiled at her.

She pushed the giggling children gently to one side and rose from the graveled walk.

"Enough, enough," she said, brushing off the dust. "You've worn me out! Let me sit with your mother for a bit and talk to her," she said as they clamored at her to come back and resume the game.

"Are you feeling any better?" Macrina asked her daughter-in-law. She accepted a cup of *mulsum,* wine mixed with honey and water, from the servant and sipped it gratefully.

Emmelia shrugged. "Not really. I haven't been right since Basil was born."

"I know," said Macrina. "I'm worried about you, and so is Claudia. Has the midwife said anything more?"

Emmelia shook her head and put her goblet of milk down. "She doesn't know. Even the physician is baffled."

Little Basil crawled over to his mother and climbed to his feet, using her robes for support. He patted his

160

mother's knee and babbled. She lifted him onto her lap. He snuggled into the crook of her arm and popped his thumb into his mouth. Emmelia stroked his hair and looked sideways at Macrina.

"There's another baby on the way," she said, and burst into tears.

Macrina took Basil and handed him to the nurse. He was no sooner in her arms than he started whimpering.

"Put him to bed—he's tired," Macrina ordered.

The nurse had the presence of mind to shoo the other children into the house, while Macrina gathered her daughter-in-law in her arms.

"It's not that I don't love children," she said when she'd recovered.

"I know," said Macrina soothingly. "You're ill, and it's hard to think of another pregnancy."

Emmelia nodded. "I've been even sicker in the last little while, and I think that's why. The midwife says until I'm keeping more food down, and can regain some of the strength I've lost, I'm to rest as much as I can."

"Don't you worry. I'll keep the children amused."

Emmelia's health continued to decline. Before long, she was bedridden, and Basil the toddler was no help at all.

"I don't know what to do," confessed Emmelia, after he'd climbed on her bed for the third time that morning, demanding games and stories and cuddles. Macrina lifted him and bounced him in her arms. He was having none of it, though, and he wriggled and squirmed to get back to Mama. When that didn't work, his face reddened as he started to cry.

"Keep him in his room until I come for him. Do not

let him out," Macrina said as she handed him over to the nurse. His cries could be heard through the house.

"I'm sorry, Emmelia—get the rest you need. We'll keep him occupied."

She spent the rest of the day with her grandson. Though he was normally a happy child, content to be with either his mother or Macrina, this day no one but his mother would do.

By evening, he'd worn out the entire household. Finally relegated to the nursery, his shrieks were at least muffled, since the room was as far from the atrium and dining room as it was possible to be.

Macrina sighed and poured a cup of wine. "Emmelia cannot get the rest she needs with little Basil constantly demanding her attention," she said to Mus. "Macrina and Naucratius are fine. She is old enough to help, and he is such a good, biddable child he's no trouble."

She looked up at her son. "What if Basil and I were to stay at Annesi until Emmelia recovers and delivers the child? It would give her the rest she needs, and Basil would have all the freedom and attention he could use from me."

Mus looked at her gratefully. "I wouldn't want to overtax you," he said tentatively.

Macrina shook her head. "It won't. I don't want to leave if Emmelia needs me, but I think if I were to take him to Annesi, it would be more help than staying here. Once she's on her feet again, I can bring him back."

Emmelia agreed, and Basil traveled home with Macrina a few days later. He was entranced by the place. Everything was wonderful: the farmer's fields, the lush green forests, and the river Iris that ran through the estate.

Frequent letters between the two houses kept each family abreast of developments. Macrina's were mostly pleasant, funny epistles, relating the growth and exploits of an active, happy child. Her son's were not so light-hearted, for Emmelia's health didn't improve. Filled with foreboding, Macrina made plans to return in time for Emmelia's labor in the early winter.

The babe, a son, was weak and sickly from his first breath. Emmelia's strength had been fully taxed, and she was slow to recover.

Her full focus was on the babe, and she had no attention to spare for her now one-and-a-half-year-old boy. He remembered his mother and resented her attention to the new arrival, causing even more problems than before the birth.

"It's been a long day," Macrina remarked one night after the children had finally been put to bed, and the baby—still officially unnamed, although family consensus was leaning toward Antony—had fallen into a doze. She picked up a ball lying against a bust of Pliny the Elder on a plinth in the dining room.

Her daughter-in-law nodded and leaned back, resting her head on the couch cushions, closing her eyes and breathing in the scent of roses in the vase next to her.

"Would it help if I were to take all the children to Annesi?" asked Macrina. "I think it would be good for them. They are bright children, and they sense that things aren't right, even though we try to make it normal."

"It would be a help," admitted Emmelia. "I can't give them any attention. All I can think of is Antony."

A few days later, Macrina and the three eldest grandchildren set off for her estate at Annesi, determined not to come back until the baby either recovered or died.

Once there, they revived like flowers after a rain. Out of the worrisome atmosphere, and in the country where there were new sights, sounds, and people, they thrived.

Macrina, following Emmelia's lead, insisted the older children, now five and four, continue their studies. She taught them the scriptures, reading and writing, and their sums. They were given passages of Psalms to read and memorize each day.

On pleasant days, once the schoolwork was done, little Macrina and Naucratius were free to roam. The villa was the center of a wide area—Macrina owned a large amount of land, some of which was farmed. There was need for a blacksmith, potter, carpenter, and baker to supply the servants, slaves, and farm with what they needed, and there was a village about eight miles from the villa. That was too far for young children to go, but they could often persuade Nona or one of the servants to take them there.

Basil was harder to occupy. At one and then two, he wasn't quite old enough to go off with his sister and brother, nor was he quite ready to learn to read and write, although he too was parroting the prayers and Psalms each morning and evening. So Macrina, often accompanied by the other children, took him on walks around the villa and her lands, taught him the names of the garden flowers and herbs, and played simple games of catch.

"Basil! Put that ball down! We're indoors. You're to throw balls outdoors, you know that," Macrina scolded as she entered the villa.

"It's raining, Nona, and we can't go out. I'm bored," little Macrina complained.

"Why don't you play **knucklebones**?" the older woman asked, brushing the rain off her tunic.

"No, we've played that already," she said. "We played it all yesterday. There's merills. Would you play with us, Nona?"

"No," complained Naucratius. "If we do, Basil will just mess up the board."

Macrina sighed. The rain was constant at this time of year. Keeping the children amused in such miserable weather was taxing her imagination to the utmost, but she kept her patience. They were remarkably good for their ages, but they too had their limits. Four continual days of rain would tax anyone's limits, she thought.

So she smiled and ruffled Naucratius's short black hair.

"I know," said the boy. "Tell us a story, Nona."

"Yes, a story! Tell, tell!" little Macrina and Basil cried.

Macrina laughed and gestured to the children. They ran to the most comfortable seat in the room and sat around it.

In the atrium, the rain chuckled into the pool as a complement to their noise, and the braziers in the corners of the room sent up warmth and slight popping sounds as the charcoal glowed from black to red to white ash.

They plopped down at her feet, with her namesake's head on her knee. Basil was perched in her lap, playing with the red woolen embroidery on her robe.

"What shall I tell about?"

"The exile!" shouted Thekla.

"Wonderworker, tell about the Wonderworker!" cried Naucratius, bouncing on the marble mosaic floor in his excitement.

"Yes," the other two chorused. "The Wonderworker!"

"Father Gregory, eh? Well, did I tell you about the time he moved a mountain?"

Little Macrina gasped. "No, Nona, he didn't, really?"

The old woman nodded. "Really."

"A whole mountain, Nona?" asked Thekla Macrina skeptically. "Really?"

"Well, a very large rock."

"How large?" she wanted to know.

"As large as this villa."

Naucratius looked at her. "Are you sure, Nona? He moved a rock the size of this house, by himself?"

"Well, God moved it, through him."

"Tell it, tell it," said Naucratius.

"I must have been, oh, about ten years old when this happened, but I wasn't a Christian yet. Gregory

was Bishop in Neocaesarea, you know. He was the first bishop there."

"We know, Nona, we know. Tell the story."

"I will, in my own way. You must understand how it was. Well. When he first came back to our city, he was one of about seventeen Christians in the whole of Neocaesarea."

"And you were one of them!" said Thekla Macrina.

Macrina laughed. "No. I didn't become Christian until I was much older. But I heard this from Deacon Nicholas of blessed memory, who saw it with his own eyes. Well, Bishop Gregory prayed hard, and he worked hard, and he converted many people. So many that they decided it was time to build a church. And you have to understand that this was a very dangerous undertaking in those days, because Christianity wasn't allowed then."

Naucratius stirred and moved closer to his grandmother's feet.

"Then how come they built it? Grandmother Claudia says we used houses to worship in back then," said Naucratius.

"And we did, when things were dangerous, but this was during a quiet period. The governor wasn't Christian, but he didn't see any point in chasing after us unless someone brought a complaint, and back then, nobody did, at least until Diocletian and Maximian took over, and the governor changed.

"That didn't mean it wasn't risky, but Saint Gregory decided to proceed, anyway," said Macrina. "And he found a builder and a place to build the church.

"First they had to dig down to prepare the foundations. They dug very deep—or they intended to."

"How deep?" Basil wanted to know.

"Oh, about three grown men deep. If your father, and your uncle Amphilocius, and your uncle Gregory stood on each other's shoulders, that's how deep they wanted to dig. But they couldn't. Most of the digging went well, but in one corner, they hit rock, much sooner than they wanted to. The builder had men stop work on the rest of the project to come and uncover the rock.

"Now, normally, they would dig the rock out, and then hitch oxen to it, and drag it away. But the men dug and dug and dug all day long, and they still didn't find the edges of the rock, or its bottom. It was as big as this villa—bigger even!"

"Have you seen it, Nona?"

"No, not the rock, but we've all seen the church Gregory built on that place. We worship in it all the time. Anyway," she said as the children exclaimed, the overseer called the builder, who looked at the rock. He scratched his head and walked all around the hole.

"Gregory's money was good, he knew, and he'd paid up to the laying of the foundations. The builder didn't want to have to give it back. But they couldn't move this rock.

"And so the builder went to Gregory and told him his church would have to be built somewhere else. Well. Gregory wasn't happy. For one thing, there was no money left to buy another piece of land and build a church on it."

"Why not, Nona?" asked Naucratius.

"Well, my boy, think about it. Gregory had paid for the land, and had paid for the construction of the building up to the laying of the foundation. The builder could refund his money for building the foundation, less what he'd already spent on digging. But who in their right mind would buy a piece of land with such a huge rock in it? Better to use another piece of land that wouldn't need such a big boulder moved. So they wouldn't buy it, or would pay much less than Gregory paid for the land. But Father Gregory, wise man that he was, didn't say no or yes right away. He went with the builder to the site, and looked at the rock with his own two eyes. He looked at it and walked all around it, and poked at it.

"'You see,' said the builder, 'it's huge. Even if we could dig it out, there aren't enough oxen in the city to move it. And even if we could find enough oxen to move it, we wouldn't have anywhere to move it to! I don't know where we'd put it. It's too large to move through the streets, and if we put it in the river, it would dam the river.'

"'Can we break it up?' asked the overseer.

"'It would take a lifetime to do that,' said the builder. 'Nobody has that much money.'

"Father Gregory said nothing. He just kept walking around the rock, squinting in the sunlight and brushing the sweat off his head.

"There was quite a crowd gathered by now—word about the boulder had gotten around, and there were all the workers, crowds from the street, and of course, members of the church all came running to the place.

"Finally, Gregory looked at the builder, then up to the bright blue sky. He stood to one side of the rock, and asked the builder to make sure everyone was safely away from it."

"And did he?" asked the younger Macrina.

Her grandmother nodded. "Then Gregory raised his hands, closed his eyes, and began to pray. He blessed God for having set the earth on its foundations, so that it should never be shaken, and for covering it with the sea as if with a blanket so that the waters stood above the mountains. He blessed God for making the waters recede at His rebuke, so that the mountains rose and the valleys sank to the places appointed for them.

"Psalm 104!" cried Thekla.

Her grandmother nodded. "Then he thanked God for all our blessings—for the sun and the moon, the stars and the sky. For the sunrise and sunset, that we may know when to labor and when to rest. For the promises He made to a thousand generations, and fulfilled in His incarnation and death and resurrection. For protection from our enemies, and the opportunity to worship Him and follow Him.

"Then he said that as God had made the foundations of the world, so firmly that they would never be moved, so were we trying, in our poor and humble way, to build the foundations of a church that would honor and glorify His name forever, to be a beacon of light to the unbelievers and a place of solace and refuge for God's children, that would stand firm as a foundation for God's light in the world. But without God's aid and assistance, it would be impossible, because the rock was in the way.

"And he said that by God's glory and power, the rock could be moved. And he commanded it to move."

She paused. The children sat, mouths open, waiting.

"And?" Thekla said finally.

"And the rock moved, and the builders built the church," said the old woman. Her eyes twinkled and the corners of her mouth twitched.

"But . . . how?" asked Naucratius, bouncing on his knees. "How did the rock move?"

"Did it fly through the air?" asked Thekla.

"Did it just disappear?" Naucratius demanded. "I don't think it just disappeared—I think it flew through the air, and landed on some awful pagans who'd been persecuting us and smashed them flat like a piece of papyrus. That's what I think happened."

"Maybe it rolled down the street, knocking all the buildings over, and scaring everybody into becoming Christians," cried Thekla. "That would be perfect."

Macrina sat, smiling at them.

"What happened, Nona? You can't just leave it like that!" her granddaughter said, frowning at her grandmother.

"Nona tell," said Basil.

"All right," she said. "The rock flew apart into pieces, and the pieces settled down into the foundation hole.

"All that was left for the workers to do was to move the chunks of rock around, and send the injured people away to be taken care of."

"But I thought Gregory made sure that nobody was close enough to be hurt," said Macrina's granddaughter.

"Well, he did, but people don't listen all the time. And God doesn't always rescue us from our own stupidity, either. The people were warned, and most did stay sensibly back, but there were a few who just had to see better, and crept up to the edge of the rock. When it shattered, they were hit with the pieces. But no one died."

"How big were they? The pieces, I mean," asked Naucratius.

"All sizes that were useful for the foundations. When God does a job, He does it right," said Macrina.

Chapter Twenty-Five
Pascha 332

It was a warm day in late spring when Mus and Emmelia arrived. Emmelia was pale and thin but obviously overjoyed to see her children again. She clung to them all, even Basil, who hung back a little and was obviously uncomfortable with her.

The children insisted on touring their parents through the villa and the surrounding area, before agreeing to go off and let the adults talk. Basil clung to Macrina, with a solid grip on her dalmatica; he eyed his parents from the safety of its folds.

They had come themselves, Emmelia said as they sat

on the terrace, partly because they couldn't bear to be without the children any longer, partly because of the memories at home.

"It got so quiet. Everywhere I went, I saw him. Sometimes I heard him. He had a little whimper that seemed to penetrate the entire house."

Macrina nodded. She remembered that cry, and Emmelia was right. It was quiet, but it could be heard just as clearly as little Basil's lusty screams.

"He's never been here, to the villa," continued Emmelia. "I thought I could get away from his memory if we came here."

She gazed at the gardens, silent for a long moment. "He went so quietly. He died at the end of March. There was no time to send for you or the children."

"They didn't really know him," Macrina said. "He is, I think, just a name to them. It would have made no sense to travel all the way down there."

Emmelia nodded. "And I was so tired and worn out that the physician insisted I rest in bed for two whole months. Then I woke up one morning and realized how much I missed the children. I wanted to hug them and hold them."

BASIL AND EMMELIA STAYED for only a month. The older children put up a fuss at being told they were to go back to Neocaesarea without Nona, since Macrina decided to stay at the villa, but it was nothing compared to the tantrums Basil threw once he understood he was leaving his beloved Nona.

He clung to her, forcing his father to pry his fingers

one by one from her dalmatica and palla. He grabbed the pillars at the door and tried to run and hide in the bushes by the inner gate.

Macrina sympathized. She was desolate at losing all the children, but her heart ached especially to be losing Basil. She had loved him since his birth, and something in them called to each other, she felt. But children should be with their parents, so she concealed her feelings as best she could and descended the stairs. Crouching by the bush he hid behind, she tried to reason with him. He wouldn't stop screaming long enough for any words to penetrate the sheer wall of noise.

"This is not how a Roman child behaves. Stop that noise now and get in the cart!" She yelled finally, to over-top his volume. He ignored her. Heedless of scratched arms, she reached into the bushes, grabbed his arm and dragged him, by main force, to his father.

Mus bundled him under his arm, climbed into the cart and gestured to the driver.

The horses pulled away.

"No, want to stay, Nona, please!" Basil begged, twisting in his father's arms, and holding his own out to her beseechingly. Macrina bit her lip and blinked rapidly, to keep her tears from falling. She smiled bravely and waved brightly as the cart trundled toward the gate, while Basil screamed and cried.

All the way through the inner courtyard and out the gates, the noise continued, bringing the overseer's wife running out of her house to see who was being murdered in broad daylight.

Macrina heard him all through the outer courtyard and through the estate gates. It wasn't until the cart had turned the corner and crested the hill that peace, in the regular daily noises, reestablished itself.

She turned and tottered back into her courtyard to collapse on a low garden wall. He was a wonderful child and she loved him with all her heart, and would miss him the most of the three children. But the leave-taking had shaken and exhausted her, and she felt her heart had been torn in two.

Valerius, her overseer, hurried up and helped her into the villa.

AT MIDDAY VALERIUS CAME RUNNING UP to the door of the villa. "They are coming back, Domina," he stammered, pointing at the open gate. "Look, there is the cart!"

Sure enough, it was pulling through the inner gateway. On it, shaken and obviously at the end of their strength, was her son's family. Little Basil, his voice ragged, still screamed.

"He wouldn't stop," Basil explained as they climbed down and handed the exhausted, but happy and now blessedly silent child back to his grandmother. "We thought he'd fall asleep, worn out by all the yelling and upset, but he didn't. He just kept wailing and crying your name."

They fed the children and let the older ones run and play, then bathed and lay in the dining room for the midday meal. Basil clung to Macrina from the moment he laid eyes on her, refusing to be parted from her.

She looked helplessly from Emmelia to her grandson. "I love him dearly, and we get along so well. In truth, I wanted to keep him here, but his place is with you."

Emmelia sighed and shook her head. "He obviously doesn't agree! Macrina, if you would be willing, it would be better if he could stay with you and come back when you return to the city."

THE FAMILY LEFT THE NEXT MORNING in the same cart, Basil dancing ecstatically beside his grandmother, waving goodbye.

Basil and Macrina stayed on the estate until the fall rains began, then returned to the city to rejoin the others. Everyone enjoyed the estate, escaping to it whenever they could from the hot, noisy, crowded metropolis. Gregory was born a year or so after Antony's death, and then several girls followed. The family grew in faith and closeness as the years passed.

Chapter Twenty-Six
Late Pentecost 340

"Nooonnnnaaaa," said ten-year-old Basil one summer evening. He entered the study and came up behind her, twining his arms around her neck and kissing her cheek.

"And what do you want from your aged grandmother this evening?" she asked with a smile.

"What makes you think I want anything? Can't I just come and give you a hug and a kiss?"

She snorted. "You can, and I love it when you do.

But you never use that tone of voice unless you're going to ask for a favor. So what is it?"

"We were thinking—"

"Always a danger with you four."

"That you haven't told us a story for a long, long time."

"I most certainly did! Just yesterday!"

"No, not for over a month. You told one of the exile stories—the one where you had the awful temper tantrum, remember? You and Papa laughed so hard at how muddy and dirty you were. So please? A story? A Wonderworker story?"

He knew her too well, Macrina thought, as she freed herself from his hug and reached for her cane. He knew she loved to tell stories of her spiritual father as much as they loved to hear them.

She moved slowly out to the terrace and sat in her favorite chair. Her namesake curled up on the terrace beside her, head against Macrina's knee. Naucratius and Basil perched on the low railing that ran around the terrace, and Gregory, five years old, crawled up on her lap. Theosebia and Julia, too young yet to be with the older children, napped in the nursery. The sun, low in the evening sky, shed a rosy glow on them that warmed Macrina's old bones.

"Have I told you about the time Gregory saw the Theotokos? And Saint John the Evangelist?" Macrina asked.

They looked at each other and shook their heads.

"When?" asked Basil. "Did you know him then?"

"How?" Naucratius wanted to know.

"This was many years before I was born. It was just after he'd been made a **presbyter** and appointed bishop over Neocaesarea. Now at that time, our city had very few Christians. In fact, when Gregory asked, he was told that in the entire city, there were only seventeen believers. All the rest were pagans or heretics."

"What kind?" asked Basil.

"Goodness, child, I don't know! There are always people teaching heresies and perverting the teachings of the true church."

"The way Arius is doing now?" asked Thekla Macrina.

"Not exactly like that, but others. There are always heresies to fight," Macrina replied. "Gregory did not feel equal to the task. He used to lie awake at night, worrying about how he could teach the faith to a city, and answer those who were so perverted in their beliefs.

"One night, he was lying sleepless, trying to think of arguments and counter-arguments to the latest heresies—and no, I don't know what they were, he never told me his thoughts, so you needn't even ask," she said with a smile as she saw the mouths open for more questions.

"There he was, worrying and sleepless, when an old man wearing marvelous, richly colored silken robes suddenly appeared to him. Gregory said he knew immediately that this was a most virtuous and upright person, who had lived a life of great holiness and humility."

"How did he know?" asked Naucratius.

"Because the figure glowed, and his face was so kindly and stern at the same time, and he had an air of strength and gentleness. Also because of the feeling of calmness and peace that came over Gregory."

"He glowed? Like a lamp at night?" asked little Gregory.

"Not quite, little one. It was as if he had a light within

him that shone through him and lit everything with a soft, white light.

"Gregory started up from bed, not sure if he should bow, or run, or quite what to do.

"But the figure spoke to him. 'Fear not,' he said. 'I am sent from God, who has charged me to bring you good tidings. Tonight will reveal the truth of correct belief to you, so that those in your care may learn and so that you may repulse teachings of heresy.' He smiled at Gregory and seemed very happy for him. 'You are to speak this belief in the city in your care.'

"He meant Neocaesarea. He pointed suddenly, and standing near him was a splendid figure—full of light, but not like the sun, Gregory said.

"'It was as though,' he told me many years later, 'she was a mirror, reflecting the light from a lamp, a softer and more diffuse light than the lamp itself, but bright nonetheless.'

"So bright that Gregory couldn't look on her, and had to keep his face turned from her as she spoke.

"It was her job, she said, to tell him that the faith they wanted him to proclaim would be taught him by John the Evangelist, who was the old man who'd first appeared and was still standing nearby. She herself, she told him, had been chosen to be the mother of the Lord whom she cherished. Gregory said later that those were her exact words. Then she disappeared, and Saint John ordered Gregory to write everything that had happened, and all that had been said, including the creed he taught Gregory. Gregory did so, and when he finished, Saint John vanished just as suddenly as the Theotokos.

"Gregory memorized the creed and preached all the lessons. Never again did he worry that he didn't know what to say, or how to teach his people."

"Oh," breathed Naucratius. "To be so close to God that the Theotokos herself comes to see you! He was very holy, Nona."

"What were the words?" Basil asked.

Macrina inhaled and held the breath a moment. "Let me think. It's been many years since I've said it." She closed her eyes and concentrated. "There is one God, the Father of the living Word, who is His subsistent Wisdom and Power and Eternal Image: perfect Begetter of the perfect Begotten, Father of the only-begotten Son. There is one Lord, Only of the Only, God of God, Image and Likeness of Deity, Efficient Word, Wisdom comprehensive of the constitution of all things, and Power formative of the whole creation.

"True Son of true Father, Invisible of Invisible, and Incorruptible of Incorruptible, and Immortal of Immortal and Eternal of Eternal.

"And there is One Holy Spirit, having His subsistence from God, and being made manifest by the Son, to wit to men: Image of the Son, Perfect Image of the Perfect; Life, the Cause of the living; Holy Fount; Sanctity, the Supplier, or Leader, of Sanctification; in whom is manifested God the Father, who is above all and in all, and God the Son, who is through all.

"There is a perfect Trinity, in glory and eternity and sovereignty, neither divided nor estranged. Wherefore there is nothing either created or in servitude in the Trinity; nor anything superinduced, as if at some former period it was non-existent, and at some later period it was introduced. And thus neither was the Son ever wanting to the Father, nor the Spirit to the Son; but without variation and without change, the same Trinity abideth ever."

The children sat silently for a moment. "That's very like the creed we say, Nona," said Thekla Macrina.

"It is," replied her grandmother. "But when you think it over, how many different ways can you say the same thing? There is only one truth, so no matter how you phrase it, it will sound the same."

The sun had dipped below the hills in the west and the first stars glimmered in the evening sky as she finished.

"It's time to light the lamps," she said. "Macrina, will you do that? And boys, you help. Sing the evening prayer, will you please? I'm too tired tonight.

"Of course, Nona," said young Macrina. "We'll sing so you can hear."

She led the boys into the house, glancing back and smiling at her grandmother.

Chapter Twenty-Seven
Late Pentecost 340

Macrina remained on the terrace, enjoying the early twilight. They were good children, and she loved them dearly. Blessings upon blessings at the end of her life, she thought. And it had been a long and blessed life—over seventy years, thanks be to God. She and her family had kept the faith, and the grandchildren would carry it forward.

How frightened she'd been the night they'd had to run! Not knowing where or how they'd go—or if they'd be caught and killed. The long years of exile, learning to live without, to trust in God and rely on His wisdom and protection. Protect them He had, by concealing them or giving them warning time after time, keeping them on the run until they'd learned only to carry His word and the relics of His saint.

God had sent the deer and the goats to keep them from starving to death. He hadn't deserted them, but had repaid their faith in Him until the measure was shaken down and running over. When they'd been destitute and lost everything they owned, he kept them fed, not only by their own industry, but through the kindness and generosity of their friends. How loving of Him, she thought. And then, to not only end the persecutions, through the emperor, but to actually give them their old lands and homes back!

He'd added joy to generosity and mercy and love, by giving her grandchildren. Six living grandchildren, and another on the way! She smiled and pictured each of them in her mind. All good children, all bright and active and healthy, praise God!

But her favorites, if truth were told, were the eldest four. Her granddaughter and namesake, Macrina. She had a brilliant mind and an insatiable curiosity. Already, at twelve, she was a gifted teacher.

Naucratius, quiet and thoughtful, dedicated to God and His service. He and Basil and Gregory would follow in their father's footsteps, as lawyers and speechmakers.

She stretched and looked over the gardens. There had been a time when she thought she'd never see this place again—she thought it had been lost forever. She chuckled, shaking her head. How little she had trusted God.

Macrina closed her eyes. She had never stopped feeling grateful for the gift of freedom—the freedom to pray openly, to sing openly and without fear, as her grandchildren were doing now, their clear voices echoing through the villa. ". . . with voices of praise, O Son of God and giver of life. Therefore all the world doth glorify Thee!"

I sang that very song to soothe my son the night we ran away from home, thought Macrina. *I love it more than any other.*

God was merciful and loving, to have blessed her with such gifts, and such a life. She sighed in contentment and opened her eyes. With no surprise, she beheld the shining, winged figure who stood before her. *It is time,* she thought. *I am ready.* She grasped his outstretched hand and followed him home.

Historical Note

Very little is actually known about Saint Macrina the Elder. In fact, if it weren't for her illustrious children and grandchildren and the things they wrote about her, it's likely that today we would know nothing at all.

We know that she was born sometime before AD 270. Her spiritual father was Gregory the Wonderworker, who is credited with converting most of Neocaesarea, capital of the region of Pontus, near the Black Sea in what is now Turkey. From St. Gregory, she learned a great deal about the faith, and honored his memory her whole life. It's said that she kept his relics in a chapel at her estate at Annesi.

Macrina lived in Neocaesarea with her husband, whose name we don't know. We aren't sure what happened to him. He may have been martyred, but there's no evidence to indicate when or how he died. We know they had one son they called Basil.

During the persecutions of the Emperor Diocletian, at the end of the third century and beginning of the fourth, Macrina's household escaped into the forests and hid for seven years. At one point, they almost starved to death, until God sent a deer to feed them. After that, He sent hinds and goats from the mountains to keep them alive until they were able to return to their home. St. Gregory of Nazianzus related this story in his elegy for his close friend and Macrina's grandson, St. Basil the Great.

A short time later, they were stripped of all they owned. Relying only on God's grace and mercy, they refused to abandon Him and their faith, and lived in almost total destitution until Constantine became emperor and issued the Edict of Milan in 313, which legalized Christianity. Because of that edict, Macrina and Basil had their property restored to them.

Macrina was very close to her family and spent a great deal of time with them. It's probable that she lived with them for at least part of her life. St. Basil, in a letter to the officials of Neocaesarea, mentions that he was raised by his grandmother, Macrina. Certainly she had an enormous effect on the oldest four children.

Her eldest grandchild and namesake, Saint Macrina the Younger, was raised and educated by her mother and her grandmother. She in turn, helped to raise and teach her brothers and sisters. At about the time of Saint Macrina the Elder's death, the granddaughter was betrothed to a man who died of an illness. The younger Macrina declared herself a widow and swore never to marry. Instead, she began to live a monastic life and gradually transformed her mother's household into a monastery. She stayed close to her brothers, Saint Basil the Great and Saint Gregory of Nyssa, influencing both of them throughout their lives.

Naucratius followed his sister and abandoned a promising career in law to become a monastic at Annesi, looking after a group of elderly infirm people not far from the family villa. A hunting or fishing accident in the spring of 355 or 356 cut his life tragically short.

After the death of his father, sometime after AD 340, Basil finished his education in Caesarea and Athens. He abandoned his studies in Athens to return to the family estate and take up a monastic life, following in his sister Macrina's and his brother Naucratius's footsteps. He traveled and learned from other monks. He was ordained a priest and became the Bishop of Caesarea. He wrote a rule for monastics which is still adhered to by monks and nuns today. Through his writings and work as a bishop, he defended Christianity against the Arian heresy.

Saint Gregory of Nyssa was a monastic but left the solitary life to marry. He taught in Caesarea for a number of years, and it's probable that at some point, his wife died. His brother Basil appointed him bishop of Nyssa in about 370. St. Gregory's writings concerned the more mystical side of the Orthodox life. He defended the Theotokos at the Council of Antioch, and he also stood for the faith against the Arian heresy, most notably at the Council of Constantinople in 381. He also wrote a biography of his sister Macrina. The Righteous Theodosia, one of the younger children in the family, also became a monastic and lived with her brother Gregory in Nyssa for a number of years. She established a women's monastery and was seen as a great help to her brother. Macrina's youngest grandchild, Peter of Sebasteia, was the head of the men's section of his sister's monastery and became bishop of Sebasteia after her death. He is also recognized as a saint.

While she wrote no major works and left no written record for us, through the witness of her life and her influence on her grandchildren, Macrina the Elder became a bridge of theology. She handed down the faith she had learned to some of the most brilliant and faithful members of the Church, whose work still influences us today, over 1700 years later. Macrina the Elder died sometime around 340, although we don't know the exact date. Her feast day is celebrated on May 30.

Prayer to St. Macrina

The image of God was truly preserved in you,
   O Mother,
For you took up the Cross and followed Christ.
By so doing, you taught us to disregard the flesh,
   for it passes away,
But to care instead for the soul, since it is immortal.
Therefore your spirit, O Holy Mother Macrina,
   rejoices with the angels!

Glossary

Ambo   In early churches, the ambo was a raised area from which the sermon was preached and the readings pronounced. It led out from the royal doors, about where our smaller ambos now stand, and reached into the center of the church sanctuary.

Amphora   A pottery storage jar shaped liked a tall vase with handles and a pointed base.

Atrium   The central receiving room of a Roman house. It was where guests were greeted and where much business was conducted by the man of the house. Most, if not all, of the rooms on the main floor of a Roman house led off it. It contained an "impluvium" or pool which collected rainwater for household use.

Caliga(e)   Roman half-boots made and worn by soldiers. They were hobnailed and of very tough leather.

Centurion   A Roman soldier who was in charge of a group of 80–100 soldiers. His title came from the fact that his group was called a "century."

Dalmatica   An overdress that replaced the tunic. Introduced from Dalmatia in the second century AD, by 500 it was the standard overdress.

Domina   A term of respect, about the same as "Mistress" or "My Lady" or "Madame."

Garum sauce   A very popular sauce made from the fermented intestines of fish. It originated in southern Spain and was traded all over the empire.

Ichthus   The fish shape, which was a secret signal from one Christian to another during the persecutions.

The Greek letters that spell the word form an acronym for "Jesus Christ God."

Insula(e)   Only the richest Romans could afford their own houses. Most people lived in apartments or tenements, called insulae, above the ground-level stores and workshops. The buildings were up to sixty feet high (four to five stories) and often cheaply constructed, which meant they were in constant danger of collapsing or burning down.

Knucklebones   Sometimes known as "tali," this game was very like our modern dice, and was borrowed from the Greeks. Knucklebones of goats were used, or similar shapes fashioned from wood, bone, or metals. The shapes were shaken and thrown, and the winner would be the one who correctly predicted the number of similar faces to be showing.

Lacerna   A workingman's cloak. Made of wool, it covered the chest and back and had a hood, but was not joined on the sides, so the arms were free.

Mater   Latin for "mother." In Roman times, the mother or mater of a household was given great respect and honor.

Mater's chair   Most Romans lay on couches to eat, although they could, and did, sit in chairs and on stools. The mater's chair was a specially carved chair for the mother of the house, and only she was allowed to sit in it.

Merills   Or "merels," a version of "nine men's morris," which is a variation of tic-tac-toe. The game is ancient and worldwide. Archeologists have found merills boards that were made as early as 1440 BC in Egypt, and 10 BC in Sri Lanka.

Mulsum   A drink made of four parts wine to one part honey. Wine was drunk by mixing eight parts of water to one part of wine, so it wasn't a very strong drink at all.

Munifex   A Roman soldier, equivalent to a private in a modern army.

Mus   Latin word for "mouse." Macrina's nickname for her son.

Nona   Grandmother—an affectionate name, like our "Nana" or "Grandma."

Palla   A long, wide rectangle of cloth without which no respectable married woman would leave her house. They wrapped it around themselves much the same way a man wrapped his toga around him, over the tunic or the dalmatica.

Patrician   An upper-class free Roman. Originally, patrician families ruled Rome. The senate was composed of members of these families. They were the only ones who could vote. Later, when the plebeian class was given most of the patrician rights, it was a status symbol marking the age of your family and the fact that your ancestors were, way back in time, actually born in Rome.

Plebeian   A lower-class free Roman. At first, they could not become members of the senate, could not vote, and were not allowed to join the army. Most of the plebeian class was made up of conquered peoples, not Roman-born citizens.

Presbyter   A priest.

Pronuba   The woman who brings the bride and groom together in the marriage ceremony. Roman tradition said it had to be a once-married woman who was still in undisturbed wedlock (not a widow, not separated or divorced). Because, in my story, Claudia had been married twice, she couldn't perform as the *pronuba* for her niece and ward, Emmelia, so Macrina did it.

Sestertius Denomination of Roman coinage, worth about one quarter of a denarius. This was in use before Diocletian's economic reforms in 308.

Strigil A small, curved metal tool used to scrape oil and dirt from the skin after a bath. Romans were very clean people, but hadn't invented or discovered soap, so they used this instead.

Toga A large, semicircular piece of cloth, white with a colored border (usually blue), which was given to each boy on his seventeenth birthday. It meant he was now a man, with a man's rights and privileges. It wrapped around the body, over the tunic, and was a privilege extended only to male citizens of the empire.

Tremis Coin in use in the Roman Empire from about 308 to 325 or so. Around the time of Diocletian, the older system of Roman currency broke down, and the emperors who followed him introduced new coins and values to try to fix things, but not much worked.

Tribune A rank in the Roman army and a man elected to represent the interests of the common people.

Ancient Faith Publishing hopes you have enjoyed and benefited from this book. The proceeds from the sales of our books only partially cover the costs of operating our non-profit ministry—which includes both the work of **Ancient Faith Publishing** (formerly known as Conciliar Press) and the work of **Ancient Faith Radio.** Your financial support makes it possible to continue this ministry both in print and online. Donations are tax-deductible and can be made at www.ancientfaith.com.

To request a catalog of other publications, please call us at (800) 967-7377 or (219) 728-2216 or log onto our website: **store.ancientfaith.com**

 ANCIENT FAITH RADIO

Bringing you Orthodox Christian music, readings, prayers, teaching, and podcasts 24 hours a day since 2004 at **www.ancientfaith.com**

CPSIA information can be obtained
at www.ICGtesting.com
Printed in the USA
FFOW02n1042231215
19578FF